"Copeland, I am not putting anyone I care about in danger. I'm not even going to worry them. I can't leave. I have cattle and work to see to morning, noon and night. And you are most definitely not going to stay here. That's absolutely ludicrous."

He shrugged, not about to let her call his bluff. He'd call hers first. "Watch me."

She stared at him, her mouth a pretty little O of shock. Which quickly sharpened into anger. "Fine." She hopped back up into a standing position, anger back over the fear and the sad. "I'd love it if you stayed, because anything is better than putting everyone I care about in danger." She lifted up that surprisingly stubborn chin. "I'll make you up a room. We'll have to pull out all the blankets. It's going to be a cold one even once we get that boarded up." She gestured at the broken windows where the frigid wind swept in.

But he wasn't about to retreat now. She'd relent before he did. "Great."

"Fantastic." She whirled away from him and stormed upstairs.

FATAL DECEPTION

NICOLE HELM

INTRIGUE

MIX
Paper | Supporting
responsible forestry
FSC® C021394
www.fsc.org

For all the reluctant helpers.

Harlequin®
INTRIGUE™

Recycling programs
for this product may
not exist in your area.

ISBN-13: 978-1-335-69036-4

Fatal Deception

Copyright © 2025 by Nicole Helm

For questions and comments about the quality of this book, please contact us at CustomerService@Harlequin.com.

TM and ® are trademarks of Harlequin Enterprises ULC.

Harlequin Enterprises ULC
22 Adelaide St. West, 41st Floor
Toronto, Ontario M5H 4E3, Canada
www.Harlequin.com

HarperCollins Publishers
Macken House, 39/40 Mayor Street Upper,
Dublin 1, D01 C9W8, Ireland
www.HarperCollins.com

Printed in Lithuania

Nicole Helm grew up with her nose in a book and the dream of one day becoming a writer. Luckily, after a few failed career choices, she gets to follow that dream—writing down-to-earth contemporary romance and romantic suspense. From farmers to cowboys, Midwest to *the* West, Nicole writes stories about people finding themselves and finding love in the process. She lives in Missouri with her husband and two sons, and dreams of someday owning a barn.

Books by Nicole Helm

Harlequin Intrigue

Bent County Protectors

Vanishing Point
Killer on the Homestead
Fatal Deception

Hudson Sibling Solutions

Cold Case Kidnapping
Cold Case Identity
Cold Case Investigation
Cold Case Scandal
Cold Case Protection
Cold Case Discovery
Cold Case Murder Mystery

Covert Cowboy Soldiers

The Lost Hart Triplet
Small Town Vanishing
One Night Standoff
Shot in the Dark
Casing the Copycat
Clandestine Baby

Visit the Author Profile page at Harlequin.com.

CAST OF CHARACTERS

Audra Young—Owns and runs the Young Ranch. Currently dealing with strange "pranks" that are making it seem like she's legally dead. Doesn't want to worry anyone she loves so she goes to Detective Copeland Beckett for help.

Copeland Beckett—Detective at Bent County Sheriff's Department. Known for his abrasive demeanor, but helped Audra's cousin when she was kidnapped. Helps Audra because he works with and is friends with her cousin's husband.

Natalie & Norman Kirk—Older couple on the neighboring ranch who look after Audra and help her when needed at the Young Ranch. Parents to Audra's new brother-in-law.

Rosalie Young-Kirk—Audra's younger sister, a private detective. She recently married the Kirks' son, Duncan. They're currently on their European honeymoon.

Vi Hart—Audra's cousin. Married to Detective Thomas Hart who works with Copeland. Mother to Magnolia. Very pregnant with her second child. Lives in Bent.

Laurel Delaney-Carson—Senior detective at Bent County with Copeland. Helps investigate Audra's case.

Franny Perkins—Audra's other cousin who lives on the Young Ranch with her when she's not traveling. Thriller writer. In Washington when the "pranks" start.

Chapter One

Audra Young didn't mind having the whole ranch to herself, even if it meant working from sunup to sundown. She didn't mind the quiet, the solitude. She didn't even mind making her own meals.

If her neighbor, Natalie Kirk, didn't send over leftovers, Audra baked herself silly and subsisted off brownies and breads. Either worked for her.

Which was good because she was losing roommates left and right. First, her second cousin, Vi, had gotten married and moved into town with her daughter and new husband. Then, just last week, her sister, Rosalie, had gone and married Duncan Kirk and jetted off on a long and well-deserved honeymoon.

Which just left Audra's *other* cousin, Franny Perkins. But Franny was at a writer's conference that would culminate in spending a few weeks in Washington with her folks.

Audra was well and truly on her own for at least three more weeks. The first few days had been fun. She got to do everything her way, which included none of Rosalie's messiness or Franny's distracting conversations.

Moving into week two of *just her*, it felt a bit lonely. She walked up to the mailbox, her usual post-workday but pre-dinner routine, thinking some company would be nice.

Maybe a dog or two to trek around with her. But Franny was terribly allergic to dogs, so it didn't seem right to get one.

Maybe she could hire on a hand. No doubt she could find a woman who wanted a little work in exchange for room and board.

But that was the problem. Audra couldn't offer much more than that. She was still digging out of the hole her parents had left her four years ago, and keeping the ranch just breaking even meant not hiring anyone on.

She paused when she opened the door to the mailbox, surprised to find a package inside. She wasn't expecting anything. Probably Rosalie sending something from Italy just because she knew it would give Audra a thrill.

Smiling at the thought of that, and her sister happily married to her absolute perfect match, Audra pulled everything out, then took the long walk back to the house.

Nothing much had changed there in the last thirty years. Her parents had never been ones for *improvements*.

Audra patched up what she could when necessary, doing everything in her power to avoid the expense of hiring someone to fix things. But that porch was starting to sag, and come spring, she'd need someone to check on the crooked gutter.

And she'd have to figure out a way to afford it because if things didn't get done *now*, Rosalie would start trying to pay for things because her new husband was loaded.

Franny claimed it was pointless Wyoming stubbornness that kept Audra refusing Duncan's overtures, and maybe she was right, but Audra wanted to know that she… Well, that she was better than her parents.

And sure, that was probably worthy of some therapy in and of itself, but she couldn't afford that either.

Back home, she scraped off her muddy boots on the outside mat, then immediately toed them off in the entry. She carefully lined them up where they belonged before making her way into the kitchen, where she flipped through the mail, then retrieved scissors to open the package.

She studied it more carefully now. It was addressed to "the family of Audra Young." Which was…weird and definitely not from Rosalie. Weirder still was the bright orange sticker on the bottom corner that read Cremated Remains.

Audra paused. Her father had been cremated, but that was four years ago, and the remains had been given to his other family. Audra was quite fine with that.

Had they changed their minds? Divvied some up? Did Audra want to know?

Not wanting to dive into those questions, she dealt with the rest of the mail first. She threw away the junk, put the bill in the to-pay pile and then turned back to the counter, where she'd left…*the remains.*

She sighed. She had to do *something* about them. She couldn't just leave a box labeled Cremated Remains lying around. Unless Audra hid it away in her room, Franny was likely to come across it and neither of those options suited.

Gripping the scissors, Audra grimaced and cut through the tape keeping the box closed. Maybe if the ashes were in a smaller container she would be able to find somewhere to hide it away. Maybe Rosalie would…want this.

Though Audra doubted it. Rosalie used to worship their dad, but Audra had ruined that when she confessed last year that Audra had been the one to do or make Dad do all the things Rosalie had given him credit for over the years.

Audra still regretted coming clean, except Rosalie had needed to know that in order to get over her reservations about Duncan. And he was perfect for her. Now they were married and happy and…

Audra blew out a long breath. "Okay, Audra. Be a grown-up." She pulled the flaps of the box back to reveal a bunch of bubble wrap. Trying not to think, just act, she pulled out the contents, then slowly began to unwrap them.

Eventually, a fancy black urn came into view. It had to be Dad. It had to be.

There was a little engraved plaque on the side, so Audra turned it over and read...

Audra Gail Young.

For a long moment, she stood perfectly still, having absolutely no thoughts in her head as she stared at her name engraved on this container.

Cremains.

And her name.

But she was here, and alive, so there was some kind of *mistake*. She had to remind herself of that in order to take a breath.

A mistake. Similar to when the power had mistakenly gone out for three days right around Rosalie's wedding because someone had called the power company and told them she was dead.

Then there were the messages she kept getting from a cemetery one town over.

Audra put down the urn, then stepped back. She rubbed at the tight band of stress that tensed in her chest, frustrated to have such a visceral response over a *mistake*. It wasn't like her.

Even when different types of trouble cropped up around the county, sometimes affecting her loved ones, friends, or neighbors, Audra rarely worried. Anyone who knew her thought she was a soft, sweet thing. And she supposed, in some respects, she was.

But she was tougher than anyone gave her credit for and had the target-shooting awards to prove it.

The problem was…*shooting* wasn't going to get her out of her identity somehow getting mixed up with a dead woman's, and Audra didn't have the first clue how to solve that problem.

She couldn't go to Rosalie. What was her sister going to do from *Rome*, where she was having the most amazing and romantic honeymoon *ever*? Audra didn't want to go to Thomas, her cousin's husband—not with Vi so close to her due date.

But there was someone who would help, who wouldn't worry. Someone Audra couldn't pretend she *liked*, but… Well, he wasn't all bad.

She hoped.

COPELAND BECKETT SAT at the desk that he shared with another detective and sipped the horrible coffee he'd poured himself after arriving at the Bent County Sherriff's Department.

Laurel Delaney-Carson was already out on a case this morning, and Thomas Hart was coming in late in order to go to a doctor's appointment with his wife.

Things had quieted down lately, which was good for Bent County, but left Copeland feeling…edgy. Too much time where his brain wasn't actively engaged left it free to do its own thing.

No thanks.

So he was happy when someone walked into his office even if, had he placed a bet on who'd walk into his office on this cold, gray morning, she wouldn't have even been on the list.

He stood. There was something about Audra Young that seemed to call for a chivalry he would have claimed he didn't possess. Cowboy-code nonsense.

He was definitely no cowboy, but he supposed she was, in a manner of speaking.

"Hart isn't in yet," Copeland said by way of greeting.

Her polite smile didn't change, but her blue eyes got a little frosty. She was the kind of woman that could be polite and frosty all in one look, and Copeland found on the seemingly soft and quiet Audra Young, he didn't know what the hell to do with it.

Or her.

He wouldn't say that she was prettier than her sister, exactly. Rosalie was a short, annoying firecracker. Audra was a slim, icy…he didn't know. Sometimes she reminded him of a statue of a goddess. All untouchable ivory. Her hair wasn't as red as Rosalie's, but it leaned that way. Her eyes weren't nearly as violet as her sister's. They were a dark, summer-sky-blue.

She was dressed in what he'd learned was the typical uniform for ranchers around these parts. Boots. Lots of denim and flannel. Hair in a long braid down her back. She didn't wear a hat, but he had no doubt there'd be a Stetson on the dash of her giant truck.

He knew she didn't like him. No matter that he'd helped find her cousin when the woman had been kidnapped. Never mind that he'd apologized to her sister when their concurrent investigations had led to Rosalie getting injured.

He knew when a woman didn't like him, because it was a rare thing indeed. Oh, he was an abrasive SOB, but women found him charming, or interesting, or a challenge.

Except the Young sisters. It was annoying from Rosalie because she was a private investigator, so she was always hounding him for information. But from Audra…well, Copeland wouldn't count it as *annoyed*.

So he smiled because he was a little perverse and wanted to see how far he could make that dislike go.

"I wasn't looking for Thomas this morning," she said carefully, shifting a box she carried in her arms. "I have a problem that I'd like your help with." She powered on before he could even register shock. She moved forward and put the box on the desk between them. "This was sent to me."

Copeland raised an eyebrow at the bright orange sticker that read Cremated Remains. He peered in the box. A shiny black urn sat in there. He might have thought nothing of it except the plaque on it read *Audra Gail Young*.

He looked up at her, already knowing the answer, but he was a detective. Had to ask. Read the reaction. "Some same-named relative of yours?"

"Not that I'm aware of." Her hands clasped together in front of her before she released them. She managed a strange gesture, almost like a shrug. "That's my name. And when I put that together with some of the other issues that have been going on, I... I know it might not be criminal, exactly." Her eyebrows drew together. "But I don't know what to do."

Always interested in a puzzle, Copeland didn't dismiss her out of hand. "What *other issues*?"

She went through them. Her power being turned off. Messages from a cemetery. He supposed it sounded like a mix-up, but it was definitely a strange one.

"I guess it's just some sort of mistake—they've mixed up my name with this poor person, but I don't know how to get to the bottom of it. I was hoping you could help, even if it isn't criminal...exactly."

Copeland considered. It was a bit of a strange gray area, and he didn't mind those. In fact, he rather preferred them to the Bent County obsession with black and white, right and wrong. If it had been anyone else, he would have jumped right in.

But this was Audra Young. He studied her. Stiff and polite. Pretty and untouchable. All Western tough girl with the strangest undercurrent of…soft princess.

And she absolutely did not like him—whether it was because of his abrasive personality, that Bent County distrust of outsiders, or something else, he didn't know. Didn't really matter. Except, he wanted to know.

"I do have a somewhat pressing question before I decide."

"Why am I bringing this to you and not…literally anyone else?" she asked, with just a *hint* of self-deprecation.

He tapped a finger to his nose. "You're smart."

She made a noncommittal sound. "Rosalie is enjoying her honeymoon, and I want it to stay that way. I don't want her coworkers at Fool's Gold to be put on the spot where they might have to lie to her. Vi's due any day now, and Thomas might not take his full paternity leave if he's handling this for me. With just about every other person I considered, this gets back to Rosalie or Vi. I know how they all worry about me out there by myself. I'd like to keep this…quiet."

"Being out there on a big ranch would be a cause of worry, I'd think."

Her chin lifted. Her eyes got frosty again. He couldn't help but smile at the attitude.

"Women have been out here on their own for centuries, Detective," she said in that clipped way he'd never heard her use with anyone else.

"It didn't end well for a lot of them."

"And that's on the male species, isn't it?"

"Or bears."

She rolled her eyes. "Are you going to look into it for me?" she demanded, an interesting and sharp snap to her tone.

He looked from her to the urn. Her name. Engraved. A strange little puzzle, and he didn't have anything too pressing going on. Maybe this would keep him busy until something big cropped up again. "Yeah. I will."

He watched as her shoulders relaxed, just a little. He hadn't realized how tense she'd been until they did. "Thank you." She tried to smile. Her mouth curved but her eyes stayed flat.

Tense. Stressed. Worried.

He looked down at the package. He supposed it *was* a little worrying to get delivered remains with your name on them.

So once she left, he sat down and got to work.

Chapter Two

Audra couldn't say that leaving the remains with Copeland made her feel any better about the situation, but it took something off her plate. And she could dislike the man and still trust him to do his job.

Everyone she knew talked about what a good detective he was. He'd helped find Vi when her ex-husband had kidnapped her. And even though he hadn't handled the case with Duncan and Rosalie last year very well, he'd apologized to Rosalie. It took a big man to do that, she knew. She was all too familiar with small men, having grown up in the shadow of one.

That being said, *no one* she knew talked about what a *good* man Copeland was. Not like Thomas, for example. Also a Bent County detective. She was certain she could survey a hundred Bent County residents about their impressions of Thomas, and the very first thing they would say would be: *Thomas Hart is a good guy.*

Copeland Beckett? Not so much. Maybe it could be chalked up to a little insider bias. Thomas had grown up here. Copeland was from Denver, which was considered a big city by most people around here. Audra didn't like to believe she carried any biases. People deserved to move into Bent County just the same as people deserved to stay or leave.

But it was hard to deny that she didn't feel comfortable

around the guy and she didn't know what else to chalk it up to.

He had an abrasiveness but she worked in a male-dominated industry—even if it was a lot of solitary hours. She helped with the agricultural society. She entered target-shooting contests. All more men than women. It was hardly that every male rancher in Bent County was somehow nice and good and *not* abrasive. It was just a different kind. The kind she'd been learning to handle her whole life.

There was…an assessing nature to Copeland. In some ways, Bent County residents' distrust of him seemed to match his distrust of them. He made no overtures, no attempts to fit in or smooth over a challenging attitude—deserved or not.

He was just…himself. And *himself* didn't seem to fit in Bent County. But he didn't leave. And he was a good detective.

That was all she needed. She didn't need him to be like Thomas. She didn't need to be his friend—it rather worked in her favor that he wasn't. She just needed an answer. And instead of turning her away, laughing at her, or doing what any of her family or friends would have done—gone into overprotective mode—he'd taken on the case.

So there was that.

She just kept picturing the urn with her name on it. It *had* to be a mistake, but that was someone's very expensive mistake. And when she paired it with the other things…

Well, it was Copeland's mistake to figure out now. She was free of it.

She really wished that was true.

Back home on the ranch, she threw herself into work. She had already spent the morning breaking ice on the cattle troughs before heading into the police station, but now she needed to work on feeding and getting the protein supplements organized for tomorrow.

She skipped lunch, because she just didn't have time for it. And if she went in and warmed up, it would be even harder to motivate herself to go back out into the cold.

By the time she walked back to the house for the night, she was exhausted and starving. Food. Shower. Bed. God, she hoped she'd actually sleep tonight.

The sight of Natalie Kirk on her front porch brought twin feelings—one of relief, since Natalie almost never came empty-handed, food-wise. And one of dread, because Audra just wanted to be alone and not fussed over.

She was on the brink of a breakdown, and she could mostly blame it on lack of sleep and food. But there was a layer of stress she couldn't seem to let go of that meant she was always a bad night of sleep or a skipped meal away from a breakdown.

But she fixed on a smile, lifting her hand in a wave until she was close enough to call out a greeting.

"Brought by some leftovers," Natalie said. "I still haven't adjusted to Duncan not being here."

Which was a lie. A kind one, but a lie nonetheless. Duncan had spent his entire adult life, aside from holidays, chasing and succeeding at his professional-baseball-playing dreams far away from Wyoming. He'd only returned to Bent County and the Kirk Ranch last year, when his career had ended. And even then, she doubted he'd eaten every meal at his parents enough for Natalie to be *so* used to making food for three.

Still, Audra would take it, as she always did, no matter Natalie's excuse. "You're the best."

Natalie smiled, but as Audra got closer, she saw a strain in Natalie's expression.

"Audra. Norman came across an issue with the fence this morning."

Audra paused midstride up the steps before forcing herself to finish climbing the porch stairs. Just a portion of her fence was the boundary between hers and the Kirk Ranch. "No damages, I hope?"

"No. A few of yours had wandered over, but Norman and Mac got them back on your side and the fence patched up."

"Why didn't he call? I would have…"

"Oh, don't you worry about that. He was there with Mac already, so they handled it. No harm, no foul. We just wanted you to know what happened. If you go by that area of the fence, you'll notice the repairs."

Ranching was hard work. Full of failures and setbacks. Ever since she'd taken over for her parents, Audra had worked hand in hand with Norman when it came to their shared boundary line. The Kirks had been like surrogate parents or tried to be. As much as Audra *let* them be.

She knew she should not feel ashamed or like she'd made some kind of mistake. These things happened.

But she couldn't keep her mouth shut. "I'll expect a tally for my half. I'll write him a check." She said this firmly. So there'd be no argument. No *charity*.

"Audra. Come on now." Natalie put her arm around Audra's shoulders. Audra stiffened against the contact. Not that it wasn't nice. Just that if she leaned too much into it, she might break. Or cry, which seemed just as bad in the moment.

"I know you want to handle things on your own," Natalie said gently. "My God, I understand it. But you've got to let us help now and again. It's the neighborly thing to do, and even if we weren't neighbors—for all your life, I might add— we're family now. Besides, it's our fence as much as yours."

But Audra knew, she just *knew* by how careful Natalie

was being, that this was somehow her mess that Norman had cleaned up, and if there'd been any way to hide it from her, they would have. "You've been too good to me."

"There ain't no such thing as too good, sweetheart." Natalie squeezed her once more, then pointed to the bag by the door. "There's your dinner. Make sure you eat it. I hate you being over here by yourself. You don't take care of yourself when the girls aren't here to poke at you."

Audra tried not to sigh. "I do alright."

"You do more than alright, but that doesn't mean I don't worry. A friend's prerogative."

Audra managed a tight smile. "I appreciate it."

Natalie made a kind of noise, as if she didn't quite believe Audra. But she offered a goodbye and headed off the porch toward her truck in the gravel drive.

Audra wished she could let it go. Chalk it up to the normal ranch problems, but with everything going on… "Natalie, what was wrong with the fence? Like, what kind of damage was it?"

Natalie stopped, considered. "Well, I guess Norman didn't say. Just that he'd taken care of it. Probably just some weather or some ornery cows."

Audra nodded. Probably, but she'd find out tomorrow. Tonight, she just didn't have it in her.

Except the idea of it being something more than accident or happenstance gnawed at her as Natalie gave a wave and walked all the way to her truck.

Audra picked up the bag and took it inside into the kitchen without taking off her coat or boots, even though she should have. She should sit down and eat something because she'd skipped lunch.

Instead, she turned around and walked right back outside. Only one line of the fence shared space with the Kirk

Ranch. It was a bit of a walk, but Audra had to see it. She walked it until she found where the issue was, ignoring the cold and her growling stomach.

It had all been repaired—with better materials than she would have used because she couldn't *afford* better materials.

She stood there in the fading light, just staring at the fixed fence, not getting any of the million things done that she needed to do.

And once the sun was down, the dark and cold steady around her, stars winking in a brilliant dazzle, she finally turned away from the fence and began the long walk home.

Since it was dark and there was no one around to hear or see, she cried the whole way.

But it didn't make her feel any better.

COPELAND'S FIRST ORDER of business the next morning was to visit the cemetery that had been calling Audra. He'd tried calling them himself yesterday, but he'd been passed around to different managing entities. Never someone actually *in* Sunrise who could get him some answers.

So he headed out to the small town and the old cemetery that felt like it belonged more in an old Western movie than in modern day.

He got out of his car and stepped into a bitterly cold morning. He surveyed the brown, desolate landscape in front of him dotted with graves, spreading out like a wave of death.

He didn't like cemeteries. Who did? It wasn't the dead. He'd dealt in death his entire professional career. That didn't bother him any. Death was a mystery to be solved, and when he could look at it like that, it didn't weigh quite so heavy.

Or at least it hadn't, until it had come knocking at his door. And cemeteries in particular reminded him of the death of too many things. Not just lives, but his entire future. Everything he'd believed in, hoped for.

All the things he thought he'd be, swept away in one moment. No, it hadn't even been one moment. Ethan getting killed in the line of duty had just been the domino that toppled over all the rest. He liked to think he could have handled the death of his best friend. It was part and parcel of the job they'd both loved.

It was the betrayal his death had unearthed that had ruined everything.

He really hated being reminded of all that. Hence why he'd moved his ass out of Denver. Not to a new city. Not even to some bustling suburb. No, he parked himself somewhere that felt so opposite of his old life that he'd never be reminded of it.

Except there were just some things a guy couldn't escape *all* the time. He moved forward through the graves and ghosts of who he'd been and headed for the little building he thought might house maintenance or records of some kind.

He didn't quite make it. His gaze swept over the area and snagged on a little lump of dirt and snow. He could only assume it was a freshly dug grave, so he glanced at the name on the bright shiny stone.

He stopped on a dime.

Audra Gail Young.

Just like the urn.

It was strange how with the urn her name spelled out hadn't struck him all wrong. It had been a puzzle, just like the woman in his office was. There had been a clear set of steps to follow. Track down who'd sent it and send the supposed remains inside to the state lab for testing. It was all just evidence, really.

But this felt…ominous. Threatening. Because when he

stepped forward, it wasn't just a name etched into stone. This had years on it, and he didn't have to look it up to know that the birth date would match Audra's. The date of death was listed without a month or a day. It was just given as a year.

The current year they were in.

Mistake? Maybe. But he was starting to think this *mistake* was something bigger. Something more sinister. It certainly felt a lot more threatening with those dates written out.

Even if he couldn't imagine quiet and soft Audra somehow wrapped up in anything sinister. But didn't he know looks could be deceiving?

He could leave his entire life behind, but he couldn't leave human nature behind.

He looked around the cemetery again. Eerily quiet. Frigidly cold.

He needed to fill out the paperwork to have that grave dug up. To have whatever was buried there looked into.

And he needed to go have another chat with Audra Young.

Chapter Three

Audra worked herself to the bone again. After talking with Norman that morning and having to practically threaten him to give her the truth, he explained the damages he'd found. He'd even taken a picture of it and assured her that sometimes when the wire got a little lax, and the posts got a little old, a cow could do that kind of damage.

Audra smiled and agreed with him.

Even though she'd felt terrified. Because the picture was blurry, sure, but the way the post was out of the ground didn't seem like a *cow* doing damage. Certainly not something she'd seen before in almost thirty years of being alive on this ranch.

It seemed like something a *human* would do. And she thought Norman would have agreed with her if she shared any of the things she'd been dealing with lately, but she didn't share. She kept it to herself.

She wanted to believe in coincidences, but they were adding up too quickly to manage. And she didn't have *time* to do anything but let that worry and stress settle in the back of her mind as she went through her day. She skipped lunch again, but she'd eaten a big breakfast so she told herself it was okay.

When she trudged back to the house, frozen through and so far past hungry she felt a little nauseous, she noted there was a car in her drive.

This time, the visitor wasn't Natalie—so no food, more's the pity. Though she did still have some of what she'd brought over last night that she could warm up for dinner. Plus, she'd pulled one of her homemade loaves of bread out of the freezer this morning, so it should be thawed enough to make sandwiches. And there was some cookie dough in the freezer she could bake.

Once she was close enough to make out the fact it was a Bent County Sheriff's Department cruiser with a man standing in front of it, she slowed to a stop.

Not just any man. Copeland stood there, leaning against his police car, the wind whipping through his jet-black hair. His gaze was on the mountains in the distance, where the setting sun made them look like golden sentries. The side of his face that she could see was hidden in shadow, but there was no denying the profile was impressive. Handsome. All sharp edges and strong lines.

He looked like a movie star. Playing an honorable but gruff police officer in the shadows of a beautiful landscape. If Franny had been here, she'd build a whole story about him. Tragic backstory for the gruffness. A shield to protect a hurting heart.

For a moment, just a fraction of a moment, really, she wondered if that was true. If all Copeland's sharp, abrasive edges were simply hiding a hurting heart. If that was why he'd left Denver and plopped himself down in the middle of nowhere, where he hadn't known a soul.

Ridiculous, of course, but the idea of the *story* of it, the *romance* of it, cheered her up some anyway, so she started walking again.

"I've been waiting," Copeland called out once he noticed her.

And right there, any romantic inklings were deflated in

an instant. *Thank you, Copeland, for your terrible attitude, clearly shielding nothing but typical* male *baloney.*

"You could have called me," she replied once she got close enough not to have to shout. "I left my cell number."

He shrugged. "I was already out and about." He turned, regarding her with those dark, direct eyes. "Figured you'd be done mucking out stalls or whatever you do by dark."

Out and about. Was he going to tell her she was worrying over nothing? Had he figured it all out so quickly that she would now feel like a total idiot? She braced herself for any and all conclusions, except…

"I'm still having trouble getting in contact with anyone at the cemetery. Through the number you gave me or anything online. But I did come across a reason they might have been trying to contact you."

He held out his phone. She had to scoot closer to him and lean forward to see the screen. Her heart did an uncomfortable jerk in her chest. There on a gravestone was her name. And…

"That's my birthday," she managed to say, though she knew her voice sounded affected. Because she *was* affected. Especially by having a death year, like some kind of threat.

"I figured," he said. He slid the phone back into his pocket, surveyed her again, but they were closer now. She could smell the faint hint of leather from his coat. "Older than you look."

She fixed him with a glare. She supposed it was a compliment, but somehow his delivery made it seem anything but. "I guess I look pretty good for a corpse too."

His mouth almost quirked into a smile, and something very unwelcome fluttered inside her in response to that handsome face showing some humor. Or in response, maybe, to just how close they were standing.

She took a step away. "There's something else. Maybe. When I got home last night, Mrs. Kirk told me that there'd been some damage to a fence."

Copeland had helped with the issues at the Kirk Ranch last year, so he knew who all the players were, and how their properties butted up to each other.

"Norman went ahead and fixed it up, because some of my cattle had gotten over onto his side. But… I don't know. It feels off. Not the normal fence wear and tear."

"I want to take a look."

"I've got a picture."

He shook his head. "Sure, I'll look at that, but I want to see it too." He gestured out at the ranch. "Show me."

She scowled at the order. Wanted to argue. God, she was cold and hungry. But he was taking this seriously, which was more than she'd hoped for. She needed to be cooperative. Not grumpy just because she'd had a long day.

But something about the idea of showing him the fence had her hesitating. Had her resenting his entire place in this. Left her with the very uncharacteristic need to needle him.

"You know how to ride?" she asked, smiling sweetly at him. "A horse, that is." She doubted it *very* much.

She watched his expression flicker ever so minutely, and only because she'd been looking for it. Irritation. But he didn't make any excuses.

"Yeah. Sure."

"Then let's saddle up."

Copeland *DID* know how to ride, no matter how dubious she looked about it.

Knowing *how* to do something and *liking* it were two different things though.

Hart had insisted he learn back when he'd first started filling in during Laurel's maternity leave. Insisted that being a detective in a ranching community meant knowing how to get around in all different ways.

Copeland wasn't one for having someone insist that he do something, but he trusted Hart. Hart might be a native, but he hadn't grown up on a ranch, so Copeland didn't think he was biased by any cowboy nonsense. It was a necessary tool he'd need out here in the wannabe Wild West. And Copeland had been bound and determined to make this job work. To make his way up to detective again.

To leave Denver and that life behind.

So he'd learned. Hated every minute of giving up all his control to an animal, but he'd learned. He much preferred the snowmobile Hart had taught him to drive this winter.

Audra led him to a building that was obviously the stables. Everything was clean, but it all kind of...sagged. Like the years had worn on it no matter how well kept the whole place was. Everything about the Young Ranch felt that way, actually. Especially if he compared it to the Kirk Ranch, which had a newer, more modern feel to it.

But he wasn't a rancher. Didn't know a damn thing about ranching. Maybe she liked things kind of old and dilapidated. Maybe it suited whatever kind of operation she ran.

Somehow, he doubted it.

She had two horses inside the building, and she went to each little stall and got the animals saddled. Copeland didn't allow himself to watch her. He took in his surroundings instead.

Neat. Clean. But there were issues. A rotted gate here, a rusted lock there. "You handle all this on your own?"

She didn't stop what she was doing, but he saw the way her shoulders stiffened. "Rosalie helps when she can. So does Franny."

"So, yes, you handle all this on your own."

She scowled at him, then led one horse out of its stall and handed him the reins. She said nothing. Then she led the other horse out and gestured for him to follow.

He gave his horse a dubious look. "You better cooperate," he muttered, then pulled the horse out into the fading daylight behind Audra.

"You need any help getting up?" she asked, with that same fake sweet smile. For the first time in all their interactions, she actually reminded him of her annoyance of a sister.

He watched with some satisfaction as her face registered surprise with how easily he mounted the horse. He flashed a grin at her. "What did you expect?"

She made a scrunched-up face but didn't say anything, just got on her own horse. No doubt her moves were a little more fluid. A kind of gracefulness that spoke to a life around horses and riding them. An innate ease with every move.

Maybe it was kind of hot. Maybe she was hot, and it was hard not to notice. Maybe he had a lot of issues. Well, no maybes there.

She urged the horse into a trot, and he did the same, following her lead as best he could. He couldn't see himself, obviously, but he was sure the difference in ease and comfort would be clear to even the casual observer.

Her braid streamed behind her, the hat low on her head. The sun was almost completely hidden by the mountains in the distance now. Gold and pastel pinks and oranges streamed up from behind the craggy peaks.

Pretty. Breathtaking, really. He couldn't deny there was something about all this space that he *liked*, but mostly his gaze kept going back to Audra.

There was something about her. He couldn't put his finger on what it was. She just…didn't fit into any easy categorizations. He couldn't get a handle on just who she was. The quiet, demure woman who stood in the background while her sister raged around. The tough rancher lady handling all *this* on her own, basically. The frustrated woman who'd given him the cold shoulder when she thought he'd been responsible for her sister's injury.

None of it melded together to make sense to him. *That's* why he found her fascinating. Once he could peg her, this uncomfortable reaction to just how pretty she was would fade away.

After a cold if short ride, she came to a stop and swung off her horse, easy as you please. Copeland followed suit and dismounted without making a fool of himself. Audra pointed to the fence. He could see exactly where it had been fixed, so he handed her the reins of his horse and got to work.

Happy to have a purpose that wasn't *her*, he got out his flashlight and looked at the now fixed fence. He wished he could have examined it before they'd mended it, but between the cattle prints, boot prints and horse prints all in the melting, blowing, falling snow…he probably wouldn't have found much.

Still, he took a few of his own pictures just in case.

"Let me see the picture of what it looked like broken."

Audra held out her phone, and brought up a picture on the screen. "It's a little blurry. Norman isn't the best with technology, but you can make it out."

He could. One post had been completely pulled out of the ground and tossed down. "Someone did that."

"Norman thinks it was a cow."

He could hear it in her voice, the obvious thread of doubt. He glanced up at her, met her gaze. "You don't."

"No," she said, shaking her head. Her blue eyes looked desolate, even in the encroaching dark. "I don't."

He had the annoying reaction to want to soothe her. But she was tough and what did soothing do for anybody? Sure didn't solve the problem.

"I'm going to need a list of anyone who might have it out for you, Audra."

She laughed, though there was clearly no humor in it. "Out for me? No one has it out for me."

"Everything that's happening says different."

"It's all just a weird mix-up."

"Then why did you come to me? A police detective. Some extensive ruse to get my attention?"

When she laughed this time, it was with humor, though maybe a little *more* than he'd been going for. Even if it was good to see her laugh. And she looked a damn sight prettier when she did that instead of looking scared and beaten down.

Still. "It's not *that* funny," he muttered.

"Right. Right." She cleared her throat and fixed a very serious expression on her face. "Seriously though. I don't know anyone who'd… Why would anyone want to mess with me this way? I can't think of a soul."

"Think of it less as who *could* or *would* do this and just focus on anyone you might have made mad. Even something that seems superficial to you. Any person who might be a little ticked off at you."

She sighed, and in the sound he heard an exhaustion born of something deeper than whatever this was. "I'll see what I can come up with. Come on, let's head back before it's full-on dark."

It scraped at him as they rode back. The way she seemed so defeated. It just…wasn't right. Out of character. Not that he knew her character. Having a few run-ins with somebody didn't mean he knew them, even if he was usually pretty good at pegging people quickly and accurately.

They got back to the stables. This time he dismounted first. When she did the same, the dismount was as smooth as her mount, but then she…stumbled when her feet hit the ground. Not *over* something, just like her legs kind of gave out.

He was quick enough to grab her before she tumbled forward. For a minute, she seemed to struggle to get her feet under her, and her whole body trembled a little bit.

He wasn't stupid enough to think it was some reaction to him catching her, but the fact he *wanted* to believe that irritated him enough to be frustrated. "Jesus, what the hell is wrong with you?"

She jerked out of his grasp, and he thought she was more angry with herself than at him, but took it out on him just the same. "I'm exhausted and starving, that's what's wrong with me."

"Well, why don't you eat and sleep?"

"Gee. I hadn't thought of that." She took the horses into the stables. He knew enough about the whole process that she had to take the saddles off and he knew how to do all that, so he nudged her out of the way. "I can do it," he muttered.

He could *feel* her wanting to argue with him, but she didn't. She watched, and once she seemed satisfied that he wasn't completely ignorant, she filled something in each stall with water and handled other things he supposed were important.

He got the equipment off and put it all back where she'd had it before the ride. They worked in silence until done. Then she shut the stall doors. He followed her back out into the freezing cold night.

"Thanks," she muttered. "Listen, I've got some food, if you're hungry. We can discuss next steps." She started walking toward the house.

"You don't want me to eat with you."

She didn't respond for a moment. "No, I don't, but it's the polite thing to offer."

Something about that really amused the hell out of him. That she was honest enough to admit she didn't want him there, but had a belief that politeness should trump what she wanted. Ridiculous.

But kind of sweet.

He should get the hell out of here. What was he doing being intrigued by *sweet*? Not his MO.

But he couldn't deny he was curious to see what the inside of the house looked like. What Audra's dinner might look like. How exactly this woman, who claimed no one would be mad at her, lived.

"Then I guess it's the polite thing to do to take you up on it."

He didn't miss the way she sighed regretfully. In fact, it made him grin. But she didn't try to get out of it, just trudged toward the house in the dark, with him close behind.

Chapter Four

Audra didn't know why she let good manners put her in this situation. Copeland Beckett in her house. Eating her food at her table. And why? Because she couldn't keep her mouth shut. Because manners her parents had taught, but not employed themselves, still ruled her no matter how hard she might try to be more like Rosalie and not care about what people thought of her.

Oh, he'd only accepted the invitation to irritate her, no doubt. He was one of those people who lived to irritate.

She could recognize it when she saw it. She'd grown up with Rosalie. She even kind of respected it, because too often in her life she bent over backward for someone else, to her own detriment.

She'd promised herself she'd turn over a new leaf after Dad had died, after all his secrets came to light, and sometimes she managed. Telling Copeland they were going to ride horses had been a needling move.

But then he'd handled the horse just fine. And thinking about the horse had her thinking about the *dismount* from the horse.

She would have fallen. Even now, her hands were shaky and she didn't feel remotely steady. She knew she needed food. She'd pushed herself too hard too many days in a row, and she *knew* better, but sometimes life just didn't let a person take care of themselves.

But he'd grabbed her. Just snatched her and kept her from falling over. He was strong. Stronger than he looked. And that was saying something because he didn't look like any kind of slouch.

She pushed into the front door, fighting between the instinct to say nothing and the desire to tell him to wipe his boots. Trying to shove down her ridiculously physical reaction to him helping her not face-plant because it had been a lot more than simple relief.

But he spoke first, after he wiped his boots on the mat and hung up his coat on the hook on the wall without her having to tell him.

"You don't lock your doors?" he demanded.

She sighed. She usually did. When Vi had lived with them, after running away from her abusive ex-husband, they'd gotten in the habit of locking up to make Vi feel safer. But Audra still sometimes forgot when she was stressed because it had never been a habit. "No one came out this way" was the old mantra.

But someone had done that to her fence, hadn't they?

"I do at night. During the day, I don't always remember."

"I'd start remembering."

She didn't bother to argue with him. Not when he was right. Even if there wasn't trouble, even if it was isolated out here, she had guns and cash and all sorts of things that could be easily swiped by some very intrepid thief wandering off the beaten path. She was alone out here, and lots of people knew it.

But they were good people, *her* people. And they weren't the ones playing these pranks now.

You hope. A horrible little thought, that voice in her head, the voice of doom.

She led Copeland straight from the front door into the kitchen and pointed to the kitchen table. "Go on and sit. It'll just take a few minutes to throw things together."

She moved to the sink to wash her hands, but Copeland just followed her, not taking instruction. *Go figure*.

But he held out his hands, like he was going to wash his too. "Put me to work. Or is that not the polite thing to do?" he asked with a grin she would *not* be fooled by. He was being irritating.

Not charming.

"Guests sit," she said primly.

"I'm not a guest. I'm a cop."

She didn't know why that made her laugh, but he washed his hands, and she figured she'd eat faster if he helped. Then she'd feel steadier. Then she could deal with this better, more clearly.

"I've got some roast beef. We're going to make sandwiches." She grabbed a bread knife and handed it to him, then pointed at the loaf of bread she'd set out to thaw that morning. "Cut some slices of bread."

"Sure."

She moved to the fridge, getting out the meat from Natalie and a block of cheese. The little tub of mayonnaise that had maybe enough for one sandwich. She didn't have much to offer in way of beverages. She hadn't gone to the store since Franny left, so she was out of milk, beer and soda. There was a bottle of wine in the pantry, but she wasn't about to suggest *that*.

Water would have to suffice. She sliced the cheese, then brought the sandwich fixings over to the counter, where Copeland had sliced the bread, but she stopped short at the mess he made of her loaf.

The bread slices were all over the place. One so thin it

wasn't even a full piece. One so thick it could have been three pieces.

"What on earth did you do?"

He scowled at her. "Normal bread comes pre-sliced."

She shook her head. "Better bread comes homemade." She put the plate of sandwich stuff next to the atrocity he'd made of the bread, then handed him a plate. "Assemble at will."

He slapped everything together in the most haphazard manner she'd ever seen. Even Rosalie had more kitchen sense than this man.

"Don't you live on your own?" she asked, appalled.

"Sure, but out in Fairmont. Where they have takeout."

She wrinkled her nose. "You can't look like that and eat takeout for every meal."

His eyebrows raised in unison with the corners of his mouth. "Look like what exactly?"

She felt her entire face heat. What an idiotic thing to say. "You know. Like…" She waved a hand at him, but she knew he wasn't going to let her off the hook. "Fit," she finished lamely.

"Fit?"

She huffed, went back to assembling her sandwich and decidedly *not* looking at him. "Yes, fit." Once she was done, she sailed to the table with her nose in the air. She would *not* be embarrassed in her own home.

At least while he was in it. She'd wait until after he left to curl up in a ball and curse her dumb mouth.

Copeland took the seat next to her, when he could have taken the seat on the opposite side. She kept her gaze expressly on her plate.

"Kind of a big place for one person."

Audra shrugged. "It's rarely just one person. Franny travels some, and it's an adjustment not to have Rosalie underfoot, but they're right next door. We miss having Vi and Magnolia around, but we all get together plenty."

"But all those fields out there. Someone came in, damaged your fence, left, without you having any clue."

Audra tried not to shift in discomfort. She didn't like to think of it like that, though admittedly the past few years had brought home just how…vulnerable they were out here.

But that wasn't just because she was a woman alone. Natalie and Norman had dealt with a *murder* on their ranch that had taken a while to solve. It was more the realization that no one was really ever *safe*.

"Yes, it's impossible to secure a ranch this size. But there's not much I can do to change that. It is what it is." She sighed, frustrated with the entire situation. "I don't understand why anyone would want to mess with me. I run my ranch. I help with the agricultural society. If I'm not doing that, I'm helping the Kirks, or hanging out with my family. I don't date. I don't party. I don't stomp around town pissing people off."

He'd stopped with his sandwich halfway to his mouth. Slowly, he put it back down on the plate. Something in his gaze was a little too…intense for her to hold.

"You don't date? Ever?"

She would *not* read in to that perfectly reasonable question. She would simply answer it. While staring very hard at the mangled bread that made up the top of her sandwich. "I did. Before my father died and my mother moved away. There was more time, more money, more…everything. I had a life back then. But not much of one since."

"And how long has that been?"

"Four years." She wouldn't feel embarrassed about it. She was too tired to feel embarrassed.

"So angry ex-lovers are likely out. Unless you think someone would have held a grudge?"

She laughed, maybe harder than she should have. "I did not leave a string of bitter, broken hearts in my wake, Copeland. I tended to be the dumpee over the dumper." Which sounded just *pathetic*, and so beside the point. She really needed to change the subject. "Maybe someone Rosalie did a case against is targeting me to get to her?"

"Then why is it your name on the urn and the gravestone?"

"I'm her sister. Hurting the people someone loves might hurt them?"

"If she was still living with you, I might look into it. But she's not even in the country. If someone wanted to get to her, they'd wait until she was around to do something about it." Copeland shook his head. "It doesn't add up, Audra. This is about you, and we're going to have to do some digging to figure out why."

Copeland finished off his sandwich, surprised at how much better it was with her fancy bread—even if he had botched slicing it. Growing up, his father had held pretty old-fashioned views about where a son belonged—and the kitchen wasn't one of them.

Copeland had grown up and rebelled in his own way, he supposed, by adopting a modern sensibility about gender roles and the like. Hilariously, it backfired, because his parents had only followed suit, and had evolved themselves, along with him.

Still, Copeland had never felt like learning his way around a kitchen more than to survive.

Tonight wasn't about *him* though.

He asked her more questions about people who might have something out for her. Ranching rivals. Someone in her agricultural group she'd slighted.

She was adamant she didn't make anyone mad.

And he just kept going back to her saying she hadn't dated or essentially had a life outside this ranch for *four years*. It should have sounded pathetic, but instead it stirred some long-buried sense of sympathy for her.

He knew all too well what it was like to feel so beaten down that life just became going through the motions to survive.

Once they were done eating, and he'd run out of questions, he helped her clear the table, then figured he'd overstayed what little welcome he had. She walked him to the front door.

"I've got some next steps," he told her, shrugging on his coat. "I'll be in touch."

She nodded and opened the door for him. He stepped out into the cold night.

"Thanks," she offered, leaning there against the doorframe. It was dark outside, but cozy light spilled around her from inside. Then she smiled, and he realized just how little she'd been doing that. Understandable, but it was a pretty smile and she should do it more. *Feel* it more.

"You're not so bad, Copeland," she said, with some humor.

But since she still looked a little sad behind it, he found himself trying to poke that sad away. "Hell, Audra, stop trying to flirt with me."

She rolled her eyes and shook her head, but she didn't seem quite so desolate. Not that it was any of his business what she felt. Not that he *cared*.

He started to make a move for his car, but something ate at him. Mostly how damn secluded this little place was. He'd been out to plenty of ranches over the course of the two years he'd lived here, and they were all like this. Felt like tiny islands of complete and utter isolation. Nothing but mountains and sky and animals, and the potential for danger in every lurking shadow.

Which he supposed was fine and dandy when someone was used to it. She was used to it. She'd grown up here. Been taking care of herself for years, clearly. Even if Rosalie had lived with her before, her private-investigator life probably had necessitated leaving Audra alone here plenty of nights.

And Audra had plenty of people who cared, so why the hell did he need to? He didn't.

"You guys have security?" he demanded, irritated with himself. With her. With the whole damn situation.

She studied him from where she stood still leaning against the doorframe. He didn't know what she found in that study, but he didn't like it. Still, she responded. "Yeah."

"Lock the doors and use it." He barked it out like an order, when he probably should have softened his words. But he wasn't a soften-it kind of guy anymore, if he ever had been.

She hugged herself, but she nodded. "Yeah, I will."

He stomped off the porch to his car and got in. Drove down the lane. All the while he kept glancing into his rear-view window. What was she doing living out here by herself? So far from any help. It was reckless, that's what it was.

He should turn back and tell her so. Insist she head into town to stay with Thomas and Vi. Hell, get a hotel room if she didn't want to put her pregnant cousin out.

But she didn't want to worry the Harts, and he understood that in spite of himself. She probably couldn't stay in a hotel with running a ranch solely on her own. And what other alternatives were there? What was *he* going to do? *Stay?* That hardly solved her problem.

Solving the case was the only way to do that. So that was just what he was going to do. And he was damn well going to trust the adult woman who'd spent her whole life on that isolated ranch to handle herself.

Because it was none of his business.

No matter how it scraped at him.

Chapter Five

Audra woke up the next morning with sunlight streaming on her face. She flew into a sitting position, glanced at her clock and swore.

It was almost nine o'clock. How had she overslept? She went over last night as she hurried to throw on some clothes and put her hair back into a tie. She'd cleaned up after her... very odd dinner with Copeland, then taken a shower, and...

She'd been so worked up about all the embarrassing things she'd said, and that stupid stumble in the stables, that she'd forgotten to set her alarm.

"I so do not have time to be so careless," she muttered to herself, hurrying down the stairs. She didn't have time for breakfast. She didn't have time for anything.

It was bitterly, bitterly cold even with the sun shining, but Audra shoved out into the freezing bright and went through another day of relentless work, with few breaks, and definitely *not* treating her body like a temple. She knew something had to give, and yet she couldn't find it.

But she made it through the day without incident. Got all the absolute necessities done just before darkness fell completely, then trudged home in the cold again and warmed up canned soup for dinner.

"I'm going to have that damn wine," she announced to the quiet kitchen. She puttered around, ate her soup and drank a glass of wine with it. She read an email from Rosalie, smiled at the adorable pictures attached. Rosalie and Duncan in front of the Colosseum. Rosalie with a giant plate of pasta. A selfie, in which Duncan pressed a kiss to Rosalie's scrunched-up cheek, some glittering Italian city in the background.

Audra brushed a tear off her cheek. She was so happy for her sister. Rosalie absolutely deserved a loving husband, a fancy honeymoon and to look just that happy. Ninety percent of the tears were happy ones. But about ten percent were the aching from missing having her sister in this house, as a partner.

Everything kept changing. Everyone kept leaving.

Except her.

She blew out a breath, set down her phone and went about doing the dishes. She wouldn't leave. This ranch was in her bones. It was her heart. Maybe some days it felt like a trudge, but the idea of leaving was too awful to bear.

So she'd weather the changes, be happy for her sister and take a long, hot bath with *one* more glass of wine. Because she deserved it.

Before she headed into the bathroom, she set her alarm for tomorrow. She couldn't afford any more mistakes. A bath. One glass of wine. Then bed.

She made it scalding. Dawdled in the water. Sipped the wine until it was gone. Closed her eyes and relaxed until the water had chilled too much to stay in any longer.

She almost felt human, she decided, as she got ready for bed. The extra hours of sleep that morning had been perhaps a *bit* of a blessing in disguise. Now she just needed to find some time to go to the grocery store tomorrow and she just might be back on track.

She *would* be back on track. Unless something else happened, like an urn with her name on it, or property damage or—

"We are *not* thinking about that tonight. We are getting a good night's sleep." She backtracked through the house and made sure all the doors were locked and the security system was engaged.

Finally in bed, she snuggled in and instantly fell asleep. So instantly, she had no idea how long she'd been asleep when she woke with a start in the pitch-black. Her heart was racing. Had it been a dream or—

Something crashed, in the distance but not distant enough.

Glass breaking, and she was too familiar with guns not to know that was the exact sound that had woken her up.

Gunshots.

And then the glass crashing wasn't so *distant*. It was somewhere in the house.

COPELAND WASN'T THRILLED by how little progress he'd made on Audra's case, but a burglary had come up and Laurel had been in court, so he and Hart had jumped on it. Because Copeland could hardly tell Hart he was busy with another case when he couldn't tell him what that case was.

Of course, technically, he could. He could rat out Audra to her extended family. It was no skin off his nose.

But he didn't.

After they'd taken care of the burglary and Copeland was back in their office, he scowled. There were no returned phone calls from the cemetery or the crematorium. No new leads to follow, and that ticked him off.

He grumbled out his goodbyes, went home to his apartment in what citizens of Bent County considered the bustling metropolis of Fairmont. Hilarious.

He heated up the frozen meal, thinking about Audra and

her homemade bread. When did she have the time? He didn't know jack about making bread from scratch, but didn't it take longer than running to the grocery store?

Well, maybe not if you lived out in the middle of nowhere, he supposed.

He settled himself on the couch, turned on a random sporting event and paid absolutely no attention to it, because his mind was occupied with Audra's case. Not *Audra* herself. He had to understand the woman to understand who might want to hurt her, that was all.

He didn't taste his dinner—there wasn't much to taste anyway. He got out his laptop and did some more research into crematoriums, the systems in place to get someone declared dead, and made a mental note to call the vital-statistics department tomorrow.

It was late when his phone rang. He glanced at the screen and wasn't sure what to think of the unknown number, well past midnight, but it was the local area code. Too used to late-night calls for work, he answered.

"Beckett."

"Copeland. Hi."

He didn't want to think about how easily and quickly he recognized her voice. "Audra. What's—"

Before he could even finish, he heard a faint *pop*, followed by…crashing.

He jumped to his feet. "Was that a gunshot?"

"I… It appears someone's shooting out my windows."

"Did you call nine-one-one?" He was already strapping his own gun on and shoving his feet into his shoes on his way out the door.

She sighed heavily, and he was about to swear at her, but at least her answer was reasonable.

"Unfortunately, yes. They're on their way, but I need you

to keep Thomas out of it, okay? I don't know how the police stuff works. When they call in detectives, and who or how, but—" Another *pop*. Another *crash*.

He was already in his car. "I'm on my way. Where are you?"

"Huddled in the bathroom upstairs. No windows. Lock on the door. I've got a gun. I could—"

"You'll stay right where you are, you hear me?"

She sighed again. "Yes, that's what the nine-one-one operator told me as well. Only she was nicer about it," Audra muttered.

She sounded okay. Not hurt, not terrified. And still he flipped on his lights and ran code. Someone was *shooting* at her house.

Played that one right, leaving her out there all alone, didn't you?

"I'll be there in…" Too long. Why did she live all the way out in the middle of nowhere? "A while. Stay on the line with me until the police get there. Were they sending county or Sunrise?"

"I'm not sure. She… The dispatcher wanted me to stay on the line, but I wanted to call you so you could stop Thomas from getting involved."

"Has anyone ever told you you're a damn martyr?"

He took her silence to mean yes. He floored it down the mostly empty highway, knowing it would take too many long miles to get there. Hart wouldn't have been much closer. Hopefully the 911 dispatcher sent someone from Sunrise. If that tiny department even had someone working night shift.

"Just…stay on the line with me. Go through the whole thing. Start to now."

"I woke up…something *woke* me up. I assume it was a gunshot, because I heard a crash, but it was outside." She sounded clear, careful. Not scared. He'd take that as a good sign. "But then…the second one. It was definitely a window in the house. Everything's locked up. I set the security system before I went to bed."

Copeland screeched a turn onto the highway that would lead him out to her place, gripping the phone between his shoulder and his ear. *His* heart pounded like a maniac, a fear he didn't want to untangle clutching his chest. But she kept giving him a calm, clear rundown.

"I knew it was a gunshot the second time, so I grabbed my phone, and got a gun out of my bedroom safe. I didn't think I should look out the window if they were shooting at them, which is the only thing I could figure would sound like crashing, so I went into the closest room without windows. The upstairs bathroom. I called nine-one-one first, then I called you. I should call the Kirks. I don't *think* they'd hear anything all the way over there, but if they did…"

"You'll stay on the line with me, Audra," he said firmly. What if someone got in? What if someone *shot* her?

He didn't like all the what-ifs jangling around. That wasn't what being a cop or detective was about. She'd given him the facts, and he was worried about the maybes.

Unacceptable.

"They're here. The police, that is."

"Are you sure?"

"Yeah, something about the pounding and people yelling 'Bent County Sheriff's Department' tipped me off. No one's made a shot for a while now. I'm getting off and going to talk to them."

"Audra…" He didn't know what to say, and she was quiet, waiting for him to say *something*. "I'll be there in a few," he muttered, then hit End, tossed his phone in the passenger seat and gunned the engine again.

It took what felt like forever, and he knew he should take a minute to take a breath, calm down. Adrenaline was pumping and he was likely to lash out at the wrong people, but when he realized that only two deputies were standing outside Audra's house, any fear of lashing out disappeared.

Two lousy deputies for a full-on shooting? He got out of his car, slammed the door shut and marched over to the deputies. Deputy Stanley was a bad cop with a bad attitude and Copeland couldn't stand him, so it figured he'd be one of the responding officers. But the other was Morris. She was a decent deputy, and she was the one who walked over to talk to him.

She clearly knew the players, because she blocked him from having a conversation with Stanley.

"Whoever the shooter was, they were gone before we got here. We've collected some evidence, but nothing that's probably going to lead us to a perp. Too many guns around this area. Victim has doorbell cam and a security system, so I imagine you'll want to start there. The shooter shot out the windows in the truck parked right there." She gestured to Audra's truck. "And the two front windows on the lower floor."

Copeland cursed. "You need to keep looking for the shooter. Plenty of places to hide. How can you be sure you looked through all of them?"

"Detective…" There was a heavy sigh. "Whoever it was is long gone. We searched the outbuildings, but Ms. Young said the last gunshot was a good ten minutes before we got here. We didn't pass anyone on the highway, so they must have headed south, or out into the pastures or mountains. There's no finding them now."

"Some emergency services," he muttered.

"We do the best we can."

It was said flatly, but Copeland knew he'd ruffled feathers he'd have to unruffle tomorrow. But that was tomorrow's problem.

"Yeah, yeah. I'll talk to her about getting the video from that doorbell camera." But what would it have caught in the dark? It wasn't like she had the kind of high-tech security that might help out. "You take her statement?"

"Yes. It'll be on your desk in the morning, along with our report."

"Alright. I can handle it from here."

Deputy Morris looked back at the house. The lights were on inside, and he could see the cracked glass of all the front-facing windows. "She shouldn't stay here. Going to get cold real quick in there."

"I'll handle it," Copeland repeated, already striding for the front door. His boot crunched on the first stair. Glass. It littered the entire porch. If he had to guess, there'd been at least two bullets, if not three, shot into each front window on either side of the door. There was almost no glass left in the panes.

He didn't bother to knock. Just shoved the front door open. Audra was right there in the living room, broom and dustpan in hand. She was wearing flannel pajamas and heavy work boots.

She looked up, exhaustion written into every down-turned line on her face. "I suppose you didn't have to come all this way." She dumped a pile of glass in the dustpan into a paper bag.

"I'll be investigating the case," he replied. "I'll need access to your doorbell cam."

"I already looked. You can't see anything."

"I'll still need it."

She shrugged, then swept another pile of glass into the dustpan. She wasn't crying or shaking or reacting in any of the ways he might have expected. She was just methodically cleaning up the mess.

It left him…unsettled. Unsure how to proceed. If he didn't have to comfort or bully, what the hell was he supposed to do?

Your job. "I'm going to look into it, obviously, in connection with everything else that's been going on."

She nodded. Another dustpan full of glass going into the bag.

"I'll read over the deputies' report and the statement you gave to them, but if you think of anything else besides what you told them or me, you let me know."

She nodded again. Swept methodically.

He didn't know what to say. What to do. And that pissed him off. He jammed his hands in his pockets, trying not to let his irritation leak out.

"I'll talk to neighbors tomorrow. Anyone who might have noticed something off. An out-of-state vehicle. Someone lurking around."

"That's a waste of your time."

"Nothing is a waste of time in an investigation."

She shrugged, as if she didn't agree with him. When *he* was the expert. Temper licked against old, softer instincts he'd thought had long since withered away and died. Which didn't help with his increasing frustration.

"You won't want to stay here tonight."

"I'm afraid I have to. By the time I get this mess cleaned up, the windows boarded, it'll be time for me to get my morning chores done. Don't worry, I'll carry my gun and keep an eye out."

"Audra, you can't stay here."

"I can't *not* stay here," she returned with a snap in her tone. "I don't have that luxury." She dumped another dustpan full of glass, and he realized just how slow going her cleaning process was going to be.

But she was being unreasonable. She couldn't *stay* in a house that had just been shot up when they didn't even have one lead on a suspect. Telling her what to do wasn't going to get through to her. He should have known that even before he started.

Audra Young required a softer approach because she was a softer kind of woman. So Copeland tried to find that kind of approach inside him.

"You have every right to be scared," he said, pleased with how calm and comforting he sounded. "Every right to be upset, but you have to think about this rationally."

"Scared? *Upset?* I'm furious!" As if to prove it, she tossed the broom onto the floor with a loud clatter. "Do you know how much this is going to cost me? Do you know how much time and effort and *money* it's going to take to replace these windows and—"

"Someone shot at you and you're worried about the *cost*?" It was the most ridiculous thing he'd ever heard.

"They shot my windows out, Copeland. If they wanted to shoot *me*, I'd be dead."

He saw it then. The first flicker of it fully hitting her what had happened, what kind of danger she'd been in. She'd used anger to deflect it, but now her hand shook before she balled it into a fist.

And she looked so damn desolate again he just…couldn't stand there. He crossed to her, took her by the elbow. The urge to soothe was painful, and reminded him of his much younger self, so he shoved it away and nudged her not exactly gently onto her couch.

"Do you know how much a new window costs?" she demanded, but her eyes were starting to get suspiciously shiny.

"Hell, the lumber to even nail it up against the cold. I might have enough in the barn, but that's a might. And my truck…" She shook her head, then dropped it to her hands. "What the hell is happening?"

He knew how to respond to this, even if knowing her meant he felt more sympathy than he should. "We're going to figure it out. They were bound to have left some evidence behind." He said it because he believed it. Had to. "We'll find it. Tie it all together. We'll figure it out."

"How much more am I going to lose before you do?"

It scraped at him, the vulnerability and sheer unfairness in this question. "Isn't your brother-in-law loaded?" he asked, not kindly. Because he didn't want to be kind or worried about *vulnerability*.

She shook her head. "I'm not taking Duncan's money."

It was none of his business. None of this was any of his business, except getting to the bottom of whoever was doing this to her. "I'll help you clean and board up."

"You don't have to—"

"Maybe your family loves the martyr bullshit, but I don't. I'm going to help. And then you're going to have three choices until we find out who did this," he said, holding a finger up for each of them. "Go over to the Kirks and stay with them. Go into Bent and stay with Hart and Vi. Or I'm bunking here." He knew she wouldn't take the last one, but hopefully it'd spur her in the right direction faster.

She laughed. "Copeland, I am not putting anyone I care about in danger. I'm not even going to worry them. I can't leave. I have cattle and work to see to morning, noon and night. And you are most definitely not going to stay here. That's absolutely ludicrous."

He shrugged, not about to let her call his bluff. He'd call hers first. "Watch me."

She stared at him, her mouth a pretty little *O* of shock. Which quickly sharpened into anger. "Fine." She hopped back into a standing position, anger overtaking the fear and the sadness. "I'd *love* it if you stayed, because anything is better than putting everyone I care about in danger." She lifted up that surprisingly stubborn chin. "I'll make you up a room. We'll have to pull out all the blankets. It's going to be a cold one even once we get that boarded up." She gestured at the broken windows where the frigid wind swept in.

But he wasn't about to retreat now. She'd relent before he did. "Great."

"Fantastic." She whirled away from him and stormed upstairs.

And he took the broom and attacked sweeping up more glass.

She'd change her mind by the time it was cleaned up.

He was almost sure of it.

Chapter Six

Audra gathered all the blankets upstairs when she should be downstairs cleaning up. When she should be doing anything but proving a stupid, *stupid* point.

Still, she was upstairs making up Rosalie's old room so Copeland could allegedly stay there—she wouldn't bet on it—because she needed to have a bit of a cry, and she'd be damned if she'd do it in front of Copeland Beckett.

Well, she didn't like to cry in front of anyone, but there was something about Copeland that made that *extra* important.

Once the room was made up, and she'd let out a sufficient amount of tears, she moved into the bathroom where she'd holed up in terror at someone shooting up her house. She didn't want to think about that. She'd rather focus on anger and pride, and never think about the sounds of gunshots and crashing glass again.

She washed her face with cool water even though the house was already getting cold. She blotted away the water and tried to blot the redness from crying along with it. Once she was satisfied there was no trace of tears on her face, she went back downstairs.

He'd made a dent in the amount of glass that had shattered on the inside. A little prick of guilt settled in her gut. It wasn't his mess to clean up, and no matter how irritated she was at him, that didn't mean she should have left him to clean up *her* mess.

Deep down, she knew there was something a little twisted about considering this *her* mess, since she didn't ask anyone to shoot her windows out. But she didn't have time for *deep downs* right now.

"If you sweep up the rest of this mess, I can get started on boarding up the windows," he said to her.

He was telling her what to do as just a matter of course without thinking it through at *all*. Guilt turned over into frustration. "You don't know where the boards, hammer, or nails are."

"Alright, then I guess I'll keep cleaning and you can go get the stuff." He said this with an easy shrug, dumping another dustpan full of glass into a new paper bag.

"Thank you for taking charge," she replied dryly. "How would I know what to do without you?"

He stopped what he was doing, glanced over at her. His expression was one of frustration, and she figured that was fair because it matched her own.

"I never said you had to clean up," she said, before she could help herself.

"What am I supposed to do? Just stand around in the middle of a bunch of shattered glass not doing anything like a jerk?"

She wanted to say something nasty, like: *if the shoe fits.* But it wasn't fair. He wasn't being a jerk at all. Just…bossy. Which was probably natural for him, considering he was a detective. And he'd been a detective at a much bigger and busier police department before he'd landed in Bent County.

She had to stop snapping at him. It wasn't like her, and it wasn't nice. She prided herself on being nice. On being the calm, even-keel that Rosalie wasn't.

But Rosalie wasn't here, so maybe she was just off balance. When Rosalie came back...

Well, she'd be building her new life as a wife. So Audra had to start getting used to life without trying to be Rosalie's balance.

She didn't care for that thought at *all*, so she turned her attention back to the mess and what needed to be done. Copeland didn't know where anything was, but she would need help if they were going to get this done before daylight. And she'd have chores to do once the next day broke.

She really, really hated needing help. Not that she *needed* it exactly. She could get this all done herself. It'd just leave her behind schedule with her daily chores, and then...when would she make up the difference?

"Leave that for now," she told him. "I'm going to need your help carrying everything in from the stables. Especially since my truck is a mess." She surveyed him and came to a startling realization. "You're not wearing a coat." It was absolutely freezing in here now, and he was just in a sweatshirt and some athletic pants that didn't look to be thick or warm at all.

He looked down at himself, as if he hadn't even considered that it was *freezing* outside. "Guess I didn't think of it."

Because he'd rushed over here to help. And as mad as she wanted to be at him, what she'd said when he'd left the other night held true. Even when he was making her angry.

He was a good guy. He'd dropped everything in the middle of the night to come out here, to investigate this case, and now he was helping her when he didn't expressly have to.

And she was most definitely the one being a jerk.

He shrugged. "No big deal. I'm fine. Where's the stuff we need? Where the horses are or—"

"Hold on," she muttered, feeling small and guilty. And

dreading what she knew she had to do. "I'll find you something to put on."

"I really doubt your wardrobe is going to fit me, Audra."

"Just wait here."

She trudged back upstairs, no righteous anger to propel her. She could not begin to express how much she didn't want to go digging through the tub of her dad's old clothes, but the man needed a coat.

She'd gotten rid of most of her father's things. He was dead and he was an asshole. Rosalie had kept some more sentimental items, but she hadn't cared about the clothes. Audra hadn't wanted to either, but…

She'd loved Tim Young in spite of it all and hadn't been able to get rid of a few of his ranch things. No matter how selfish he'd been, no matter how much of a liar he'd been, he hadn't *always* been a terrible father. He'd taught her how to ranch with a patience and reverence that stuck with her still.

She went into her room, opened the closet, pulled out her little step stool and got on it, so she could reach the back of the top shelf. She pulled down the tub and opened it up. The smells of tobacco and soap and horses hit her like another blow.

For a moment, she squeezed her eyes shut and willed the tears away. She'd already cried. No time for another one. She jerked the work coat out of the bin, some gloves, a stocking cap. She didn't have anything for Copeland to put on over the pants, not that pants would fit. Dad had been a lanky beanpole. Copeland was probably just as tall if not taller, but he was sturdy.

So she went to her drawers, and did not let herself think about how *sturdy* Copeland's body was. She'd kept a bunch of Dad's wool socks to wear herself on winter mornings, even though they were too big. She pulled out a pair and then headed back downstairs, doing everything she could not to let the old smells transport her back to a time when everything hadn't fallen on her shoulders.

Except, even then, she'd taken on more than her fair share for a kid. She'd wanted to give Rosalie the image of a perfect family. Find a way to make Rosalie feel loved by their parents, when Audra had never been sure they even knew how to love. Not their kids, and certainly not each other.

Hadn't stopped Dad from starting a secret second family, of course. She'd tried reaching out to her half siblings when she'd discovered they existed after he died. She'd wondered, did they feel the same? Or…was she just that hard to love?

And with *that* awful and not at all helpful thought, she arrived back downstairs and shoved the pile of clothes at Copeland. "You'll still be cold, but this'll help."

He lifted an eyebrow. "Keep a lot of menswear around?"

She could say yes and leave it at that, but she didn't want him making any more comments about it. "They were my father's. He's dead, so he's not using them."

Copeland opened his mouth, but nothing came out. It was a little bit of a win for the day, to make Copeland Beckett speechless even if it was over something she wanted to stop thinking about.

"Put it on, Copeland. We've got work to do."

It took all night. The sun was creeping up over the horizon by the time the glass was cleaned up, inside and out, and the broken windows boarded up.

Copeland had insisted on cleaning out her truck while she swept the porch. He was just about done, just needed to tape up some plastic over the windows so no precipitation got in before she had a chance to get the windows fixed.

He was tired if he stopped to think about it, and very hungry, but it wasn't like he'd have gotten any sleep if he'd gone home. Plus, she'd still be working on this.

He'd have thought the porch sweeping could wait, but she was worried about wild animals, of all damn things. Once she'd finished bagging up the glass from the porch, she came over to help him.

But he figured she'd done enough. "Don't worry about this, I'll finish. Why don't you go on up to bed? I've got my computer in my car. I'm going to grab it and see if Morris sent me the report. I can work from out here for a bit."

"You don't have to do that."

Even though the automatic dismissal grated, he saw it for what it was. Knee-jerk. Not about *him* most of the time. Maybe it was incomprehensible to him that she lived out here all on her own—or with her sister or cousins, though he saw no evidence they were big parts of the *ranch* life Audra had going on. But it was her life, and she was simply used to handling things on her own.

"How about this? We make an agreement. You stop telling me I don't *have* to do things, and I won't have to waste my breath telling you not to waste yours. I'm not going anywhere if you're not. Not until we find the shooter."

She didn't say anything for a few humming moments. He knew she waged some kind of war with temper, and he didn't think temper was a usual part of her life, but what did he know?

Not a damn thing about her, and that was just fine.

You know she can bake bread, hasn't dated in four years, holds too much on her shoulders, smells like lilacs at the strangest times. Dead dad, annoying sister. Expressive blue eyes a shade you can't quite match to anything.

"I'll make some breakfast," she finally said, saving him from the ridiculous turn of his thoughts.

"You need to get some rest."

She shook her head. "I'm starving. I've got some stuff already prepared. Just need to warm it up and get the coffee on."

"Alright. I'll finish this."

He watched her hesitate. No doubt she wanted to do it all on her own. Hell, he should let her. It was none of his business if she wanted to work herself into an early grave.

But after that moment of hesitation, she walked away and went inside. Copeland finished taping up the plastic cover. He collected the tools, figuring he might as well get some breakfast before he grabbed his laptop and got to work, but as he turned, he stopped.

In the east, the sun rose. He was frozen to the bone, and yet he couldn't quite force himself to go inside. The sky was a riot of colors as the light reached up its bright fingers and shimmered, changing the sky from night to day in an awe-inspiring display of pure beauty.

He'd seen his share of natural beauty since moving to Wyoming, even back home in Denver. The mountains. Sunrises and sunsets. The West was full of pretty landscapes he'd spent his entire life seeing.

But this was something else. Less a landscape and more a vibrancy that seemed to pull at something deep inside of him. It was strangely poignant, a feeling he couldn't quite ever remember settling over him, and he was afraid if he inspected that feeling too deeply, it'd be something too close to *belonging*. When he hadn't moved to Bent County—the middle of nowhere—to *belong*. In fact, quite the opposite.

So he turned away from the pretty sunrise that was *just* a sunrise. Same as the sun rising anywhere else. There were mountains in plenty of places. Nothing special about these.

He headed inside, following the smells of coffee and cinnamon into the kitchen.

It was very nearly warm in here. Maybe he could imagine taking off the coat she'd loaned him. Oh, in an hour or so.

It was some kind of strange homey picture, even with her bundled up against the cold. She moved around the kitchen with the same efficient certainty she did everything. Her braid swung with each movement. She moved a pan of some kind of frosted roll onto the table.

"Sit. Eat," she instructed. Two plates and two forks were already set out, and she moved back into the kitchen, pouring coffee into two mugs.

The *two* of it all was really messing with his equilibrium. Because he'd been here before. Not *here* here, but he had a whole other life of being a *two*, and he'd moved here to leave it the hell behind.

Since he was feeling unmoored, he didn't know what else to do but follow instructions. Besides, he was frozen and starving. Why not sit and eat? Audra wasn't his ex-wife or anything else. They were no couple. So he should stop being an idiot.

He took a sip of coffee first, nearly closed his eyes and groaned in appreciation. Warmth. Caffeine. Then he helped himself to two giant, gooey cinnamon rolls.

After the first bite, he pointed his fork at her in accusation. "These did not come from a can."

Her mouth curved, ever so slightly. "No, I make big batches from scratch, then freeze them. Then you just have to cook them and thaw the frosting."

"There shouldn't be a *just* in that sentence. That's got to be a ton of work. Far more work than separating a log of dough and tossing it on a pan."

"Maybe, but the reward is worth the work. Besides, baking is fun. A hobby, I guess."

"You would have a hobby that was probably more for other people than yourself."

He could tell she didn't like that observation by the way she scowled briefly before smoothing it out into that haughty, chin-in-the-air expression of hers.

"My other hobby is shooting things," she said coolly.

He tried to picture her shooting *anything*. Couldn't. "I know word on the street is you can handle your own, but I cannot even begin to visualize it."

"I'll give you a demonstration."

He grinned in spite of himself. "Sounds hot."

She snorted, clearly in spite of *herself*. Then shook her head. She ate a few bites, sipped her coffee and kept her eyes on the unbroken window on the other side of the table that looked out over her ranch.

He didn't *know* her, but it didn't take a psychic to watch her gaze and know she was making a mental list of everything she had to do today. When she *needed* sleep. He didn't exactly know his way around a cattle ranch, and it was certainly none of his business if she got rest or not, but… It was just the sensible thing to do to offer a hand.

In fact, it *was* sensible. Someone was targeting her, and if he stuck close, maybe he'd catch whoever was trying to scare her. She wouldn't accept *that*, so he'd offer to help. Not that she'd accept that, either, but he'd push until she did.

"Since I'm going to be staying here, you should put me to work."

Her gaze whipped to his, sharp and irritated. "You are *not* staying here."

"Good. You've come to your senses. I'll help you pack so you can go stay with Hart."

"I'm—" But her furious retort was cut off by a loud knock on the door. She pushed back from the table, muttering as she went to answer it.

He doubted the shooter was *knocking on the door*, but he followed her anyway, casually resting his hand on the butt of his weapon.

She opened the door to an older woman he recognized because he'd worked on the murder at the Kirk Ranch last year.

"Natalie," Audra greeted, surprise tinging her tone. And maybe embarrassment. "Uh. Good morning."

"I came as soon as I heard. Why didn't you call?" She engulfed Audra in a tight hug. "Oh. I see," the woman said, her eyes meeting his across the room.

Copeland stood in the doorway between kitchen and living room, pinned by the older woman's steady gaze.

It was obvious what Mrs. Kirk was thinking—which was *hilarious* considering why he was here. Considering what Audra thought of him.

And what you think of her, right?

"Morning, Mrs. Kirk," he offered, as Audra turned to look at him. Embarrassment was etched into her gaze.

"Morning, Detective."

"Copeland is investigating everything," Audra said. And he didn't miss the way she used his first name, the way she imbued it with a kind of familiarity they didn't *really* have. Because she didn't sound irritated and like she wanted to prove she could shoot things with him as a target.

Quite the opposite.

"He's sticking around during the investigation. You don't need to worry about me, Natalie."

Mrs. Kirk's gaze moved from Audra to Copeland. "I'm glad you're here watching over our Audra." She gave Audra another squeeze. "You can ask us for anything. And if Copeland can't be around, you know we've got room and all those safety measures Duncan put in place last year. You can depend on us."

"I know. I do. But it'll be easier if I stay put, and Copeland will…be here."

"Good," Mrs. Kirk said firmly. She glanced at the boarded-up windows, her expression one of concern.

Why Audra couldn't suck it up and take her friend's concern *baffled* him.

"Natalie… If Duncan and Rosalie call, please don't mention this. Let them enjoy their honeymoon. They deserve it."

Mrs. Kirk's mouth firmed. She clearly didn't *like* the request, but eventually she nodded. "As long as it's cleared up in a few days. If it's not, no promises. Your family deserves to know when you're in danger, when you need help."

Audra nodded along, but he knew she didn't agree. It was written all over her stiff posture. "Sure, but I've got Copeland," she said.

He wanted to laugh. What a *liar* she was. She'd just tried to kick him out a few minutes ago. He wondered what made this woman so determined to reject help. He understood from *him*. But her own friends? Family? What the hell was that about?

"Be safe, Audra," Mrs. Kirk said, hugging Audra close to her, and giving Copeland a look like "you better take care of her."

And, because he didn't know what the hell else to do, he nodded like he would.

Mrs. Kirk stepped back, gave Audra a wave and left. Audra closed the door, but didn't move. Didn't turn to face him. She just stood there, back to him.

He could have let it go. He *should* have let it go. But he couldn't deny he was shocked that she'd let Mrs. Kirk think anything was happening between them. He'd have thought her pride would be too big to handle the weight of such an outright lie.

"You let her think we're sleeping together."

Her shoulders slumped a bit as she turned and leaned back against the door. He watched with more fascination than he should have as her cheeks turned a deep shade of pink. "She won't worry so much if she thinks you're hanging around for...personal reasons," Audra muttered.

"And heaven forbid anyone worry about you?"

Her chin came up. "I've been taking care of myself for a long time."

Yeah, he didn't doubt it. And it was certainly none of his concern, not his responsibility to swoop in and take some of those weights.

But he was *here*. "Put me to work, Audra."

Chapter Seven

Audra didn't want Copeland underfoot. She was convinced he'd be more hindrance than help.

She should have known better. Everything she told him to do—mostly grunt work that required little more than muscle and following directions—he did. Easily. Efficiently. Without complaint. Quite the improvement on Rosalie, who helped when she had time, but didn't *enjoy* ranch work and liked to be verbal about that.

Except when she was feeling guilty about how much Audra did. Then she'd try to keep her mouth shut, and that was always worse. Because Rosalie's guilt made Audra feel guilty, and like she had to prove just how much more she could handle it all on her own.

She was too exhausted today to even convince herself this wasn't easier. If she didn't have Copeland helping, she would have spent *weeks* recovering from how far behind she'd be. She likely would have *had* to ask Norman for some help.

And then Duncan and Rosalie would have tried to convince her *they* should hire some help, because *they* had the money to spare, and it was a *family* ranch.

Except she was the only one who cared about the ranch. So why should she accept their pity money? She could do this on her own. She *was* doing this on her own. This was just a blip because…

Someone…wanted to scare her for some reason.

She just wished she had any inclination about *who* would want to scare her and make her life harder. The fact that she couldn't think of anyone left her feeling…stupid. Was she that naive? Thinking most people she dealt with liked her or didn't think of her at all?

She glanced at Copeland as they walked back to the house. It was early yet, but the sun was setting and he'd made some complaints about her wandering around after dark. Complaints she couldn't quite argue with.

Especially since he hadn't complained about working through lunch. Hadn't asked for a break or said he had to go do his own work. He'd actually been…the perfect help today.

How annoying. "I guess you're a natural," she told him. "For a city boy."

He grinned at her, and that wasn't fair. The way that grin crinkled his eyes and softened the harshness of the sharp angles of his face. The way it seemed to dance inside of her, far too close to attraction for her to accept.

"Actually, I grew up in the suburbs," he said. "Moved to Denver when I got a job with the PD."

"You know, to us folks out here, city and suburbs is essentially all the same."

He looked around, and she didn't know what he felt when he took in the mountains, the pastures, the vast, never-ending landscape. "Guess that's fair, all in all."

He stopped abruptly, and when he did, she heard the faint putter of an engine coming up the drive. Copeland put an arm in front of her to stop her forward movement, and she noted his other hand went to the weapon she hadn't fully realized he'd kept on his hip, because it was hidden under her father's coat.

When the car came into view though, Audra recognized

it. "It's just Thomas and Vi." But Audra didn't move forward as a terrible thought took hold. "You told them," she accused.

He shook his head, expression grim. "No, I didn't. But there was no keeping it on the down-low at Bent County, Audra. It might be a growing department, but everyone knows everyone. And people love to gossip. If Hart was in the office today, he heard about it."

He started moving forward, and Audra followed. Should she feel guilty for accusing him? She didn't have time to fret over it, because the minute Thomas put Magnolia down on the ground, she was squealing in delight.

"Aud-da!" Magnolia yelled and came running toward her. The enthusiastic greeting had Audra smiling, and she kneeled down so she could accept and return Magnolia's happy, sticky hug.

For a moment, she closed her eyes, inhaled the scent of the toddler and let herself relax. She missed having this little bundle of enthusiastic energy under her roof, even if she was happy for the new life Vi and Magnolia were building.

She stood, hefting Magnolia with her. Vi and Thomas were both frowning at the boarded-up window as they approached Audra and Copeland in front of the porch. Audra didn't dare look at Copeland.

Vi was smiling as she waddled up, hand on her belly. Thomas carried a couple boxes of what was clearly pizza.

"We brought some dinner. Thought we could all eat together."

"Pizza pah-ty!" Magnolia shouted, wriggling happily in Audra's arms.

"Well, you're speaking my very hungry language. Come on inside."

"We'll be right in," Thomas said, handing the pizzas off to Vi. He smiled at Audra, but she saw the tension in his expression. It made her nervous that he wanted to talk to Copeland alone, but Vi and Mags shouldn't be out here in this cold.

So she led them inside. Settled Magnolia on a chair and then set about getting plates and cups together.

"I'm sorry we didn't give you advanced warning, but… Audra." Vi stopped Audra's forward movement by stepping in front of her. "Why didn't you tell us?"

Audra sighed. "Vi." She placed a gentle hand on Vi's giant belly. "You take care of you and yours. I'm just fine."

"You are part of that *yours*," Vi said fiercely, putting her hand over Audra's. "Someone shot at you."

"No, they shot at the house." Audra took her hand back and gestured for Vi to sit down. "Broke some windows, which is all they were trying to do. They didn't try to break in. They didn't try to shoot me."

"Oh, well, I feel *so* much better," Vi muttered, taking a seat as Audra put a piece of pizza on a plate for Magnolia and began to cut it into toddler-size pieces.

"Who would want to scare you like that?" Vi demanded.

Audra thought of the urn, the gravestone, all the other issues. "I really don't know."

"Come stay with us, Audra. I know you've got chores, but it's so much easier to keep someone safe in town, in a smaller house."

Audra didn't point out that Vi had been kidnapped from the very house she now lived in, even though she wanted to. But she didn't want to remind anyone of how scared they'd all been.

"Vi, you're going to be induced tomorrow if you don't pop today." She filled a sippy cup—something she kept on hand just for Mags—with some of the chocolate milk Vi had brought, then went to fix Vi a plate. "So what are you going to do from a hospital bed?"

"Thomas will—"

"Be by your side and take his paternity leave. Copeland is handling this. You're always telling me he's a good detective and not as unfriendly as he seems."

Vi sighed and looked into the living room, where Copeland and Thomas were coming in the door, talking in very low tones. "He *is* a good detective, and a good guy, under all that gruff. But… Come stay in town. I don't like you out here so isolated."

"I have too much to do on the ranch." She put Vi's plate in front of her, plus a glass of milk. "Besides, Copeland has got it in his head to play personal bodyguard until they have a suspect." She filled her own plate, then sat next to Magnolia.

Vi leaned forward, something sparkling in her eyes that left Audra feeling…uneasy. "How *personal*?" she asked, with *some* excitement.

Audra felt her cheeks heat and she wrinkled her nose. "It's not like that."

Vi leaned back and sighed. "Too bad."

"Too bad?" Audra looked out at where Thomas and Copeland were talking in front of the boarded-up window. No doubt about the shooting. "He is so not my type."

"You're too busy to have a type. Besides, what's not to like?"

"He's bossy, overbearing, never compromises?"

"Sounds like literally everyone in your life that you love."

Since she desperately wanted to change the subject, and it brought up a new one, it was Audra's turn to lean forward. "Don't tell Rosalie if you talk to her."

"Audra."

"She shouldn't cut her honeymoon short for this, and she would. And for what? So she can storm around shooting right back and making things more complicated?"

Vi pulled a face, rubbed the side of her belly. "I'll think about it, but I'm not making any promises."

THEY ATE DINNER and didn't discuss the shooting or the threats. Hart didn't come out and say it, but Copeland got the impression that he hadn't shared *all* the details with his wife.

So they talked about baby names and paternity leave and so much family stuff Copeland wanted to jump out of his own skin.

He didn't do family stuff. He could go for a beer with Hart and hear about the kid, or even listen to Laurel and Hart yammer on about family life at work, but doing it at a family kitchen table just made everything…awful.

There'd been a time he thought this would be his future. The wife. The kid. The dinners at a kitchen table, just like he'd grown up with. It was long ago enough that it shouldn't still cut like a rusty blade, but it damn well did.

When Magnolia gleefully knocked over her cup of milk, Copeland faked a phone call and stepped out of the room. Into the cold night. Until he could breathe.

But before he could go back in, the front porch light flicked on and the whole crew spilled out of the front door in noisy, cheerful exuberance.

Audra was carrying Magnolia, and Vi was laughing about something she'd said. But Hart jerked his chin toward Copeland's cruiser, and started walking that way, so Copeland followed him.

"You're sure you're good with staying? At least until Vi's out of the hospital. Our parents are coming, so I've got help. I can take a turn or two out here. I can—"

"Take care of your family, Hart," Copeland said, irritated at how sharp his voice sounded. "I've got this handled." He glanced at the two women standing in the dim glow of the porch light.

They made quite the pair. Vi's hair was reddish brown, just like Audra's. Even with the big baby bump, she had a... fragile air about her. Copeland knew Vi's story—abusive ex she'd escaped, twice—so he knew she was tough, but she didn't have the *look* of toughness about her. Not like Audra did.

Audra had little Magnolia on her hip while she spoke to Vi, who looked huge and uncomfortable and reminded Copeland of too many things he'd left behind.

So Copeland forced his gaze onto Hart. And, in spite of himself, tried to soothe his worry. "This stuff, it's all connected. But it's all...weird, petty stuff. You guys don't need to worry. I'll figure it out."

Hart only frowned. "A gravestone feels more threatening than petty."

"I'd agree, but they shot to destroy. Not to hurt."

"It hurts."

"You know what I mean." He glanced back at Audra. Couldn't seem to stop himself. "She can't think of anyone, not *anyone*, who'd want to mess with her. Who doesn't at least have one enemy?"

"Audra Young."

Copeland grunted. "She suggested someone after Rosalie. It makes more sense on paper, but in reality..."

"This is all really personal."

"Yeah."

Hart sighed. "Maybe this goes without saying, but since I'm going to be focused on my wife tomorrow, I have to say it. Audra's my family, even if it's only by marriage. If anything happens to her..."

"I've got it handled. She doesn't want me here, but I'm not leaving. Blood on my hands isn't my MO."

"Yeah, that all it's about?"

Copeland didn't stiffen, though he wanted to. "What else would it be about?"

"You're not exactly a monk."

"Yeah. Exactly. I'm not looking for serious. Audra Young's got serious written all over her. This is just a job, and a favor to a few friends who consider her family."

"It's not so bad," Hart said, in that gentle way of his that always made Copeland feel itchy. "Serious. Family."

Copeland only grunted. Hart clapped him on the back.

"I'm counting on you, Copeland."

Copeland didn't consider himself part of any community. He didn't make friends anymore. Didn't get involved in people's lives. He'd left that behind in Denver.

Or so he'd thought. Because it struck him as a surprise, just how much that *counting on* weighed.

Because Hart was his friend, and Copeland didn't want to let him down. He watched as Hart moved over to the group, took Magnolia out of Audra's arms, smiled, chatted. Then wrapped his free arm around his wife and moved her to the car.

They got in with waves and goodbyes, leaving Copeland in the yard and Audra on the porch. Alone, essentially, together in the dark.

"Moved to this damn place so I wouldn't have any ties, and here I am all tied up," he muttered to himself, turning to walk over to the porch.

But apparently she wasn't on the porch. She was right there.

"Why didn't you want any ties?" she asked, tilting her head and studying him even though dark hung around them.

Irritated with himself, he shrugged, tried to be casual. "Long story."

"Seems like we've got a lot of time for a long story since you insist on being underfoot."

"Seems like," he agreed, moving for the house. "But not tonight. You haven't slept a wink."

Instead of admitting that was true, she got all stubborn about it. "Neither have you," she said, following after him.

"Used to it. Life of a cop."

She moved in front of him, stopped his forward movement by planting herself in front of the porch, fisting her hands on her hips. "Well, *I'm* used to it. Life of running a ranch on my own."

"Are you always this stubborn or is it just on my account?"

She huffed. But he was a cop. He knew how to deescalate a situation and knew that was absolutely not what he was doing right now.

But he didn't seem to care. Neither did she.

"I grew up with Rosalie," she retorted. "*I* am not stubborn. *I* make compromises. You're inexplicably here, aren't you? Doing chores and cleaning up messes that aren't yours. If I was stubborn, or more stubborn than you, I'd be the one doing all that."

"They aren't your messes either. In fact, as the investigating detective, it's more mine than yours."

She threw her arms up in the air. "That's ridiculous."

"*You're* ridiculous." And he was tired, no doubt, which was the only reason he snapped. Why else would he be so easily irritated? "You've got person after person coming here, worried about you, wanting to help you, and you just shove them all away."

"Oh, because a normal person would want their family and friends in the line of fire?"

"A sensible person takes help. A *sensible* person knows when they're out of their depth."

"Out of my *depth*?" She all but screeched it. He was actually kind of fascinated, watching her temper fracture. She even reached out, as if to give him a little shove, but instinctually, he gripped her hands to stop her from landing it.

They stood there, too close. Her hands on his chest, his hands curled over her wrists. Connected with moonlight settling over them like a blanket. Both looking at each other, both breathing a little too hard.

He wasn't thinking about how mad he was anymore. He didn't think she was either.

Which was…dangerous.

He dropped her hands. Sidestepped her block of the porch. "Well, *I'm* going to use my sense and go get some sleep. Don't forget to lock up." Then he marched his frozen ass inside, determined that he wasn't doing any chores tomorrow.

He was finding a shooter.

Chapter Eight

Audra considered it lucky that she slept. Exhaustion won out over anger.

And all the other things storming around inside of her.

The problem was, when she woke up to her trilling alarm the next morning, they were all still right there. Anger less than before, but the other things…

She shut off the alarm, then lied back in bed and stared at the ceiling and scowled. It grated that she found him attractive, that she had a *physical* reaction to him. She didn't want that.

But it had shimmered through her, twining with frustration, last night on the porch. She didn't know what had come over her. She'd just…needed to act out. Give him a little shove. Not to *hurt*. She wasn't a violent person. She just wanted to prove a point.

Instead, he'd stopped her, put his big, rough hands around hers, and then held them there. In the frigid night with starlight dancing around them.

And her body had felt too many things at once—a warmth that shouldn't have existed on a cold winter night, a shudder deep inside that seemed to awaken old desires she'd pushed way, way, *way* down under responsibility, and the thrill of something she didn't want at all.

Unpredictability. Surprise. Uneven footing.

No matter what her body thought of that, her brain knew better. *That* was a recipe for heartbreak and disaster.

She'd love to live in denial, but that didn't get her anywhere. She was attracted to Copeland, and that was annoying with him underfoot. Because she wasn't about to do anything about that attraction. She didn't want anything to do with the man, even if he was hot.

Her perfect guy was kind and quiet. The stoic rancher type with a squishy heart of gold. They'd take care of the ranch together. He'd know how to cook. She'd bake. They'd have kids and a dog and a nice, quiet, happy, *predictable* life. She hadn't met him yet, and maybe she never would, but she definitely didn't want a grumpy, arrogant *detective* from the city who'd probably never been predictable a day in his life.

So why did she find herself reliving that moment like it was some kind of romantic overture from one of the romance books or movies she loved?

He'd stopped her from pushing him. The end.

She rolled onto her stomach, groaned into her pillow. It was five seconds of indulgence, and now she had to get up and get moving. She still needed to do something about her truck…at some point.

She didn't know where the money was going to come from. She might actually have to accept some help from Rosalie, which left her feeling grumpier than being attracted to Copeland did.

She got dressed and trudged downstairs, but she stopped short halfway across the living room. She smelled…coffee. Even when Rosalie and Franny were here, she was always the one to get up and make coffee. Except on the rare occasions Franny pulled an all-nighter to meet a deadline, but even then, the coffee was usually old and bitter.

She gave a fleeting thought to retreating, but that was

cowardly, and more than that, she couldn't skip breakfast. Not when she had so many chores to do *and* figure out how she was going to get up to the hospital once Vi had the baby.

Maybe her truck was drivable. Sure, it didn't have windows, but she could bundle up. Maybe.

That was a problem for later. First, she needed coffee and breakfast. So she powered forward, into the kitchen, where Copeland already was.

He stood at her sink, his back to her. He was looking out the window. Beyond his silhouette, the sun was starting to make the mountains glow gold, even as the immediate world around the house remained dark.

For a moment, she had the strangest sensation of déjà vu. Like she'd seen this exact moment before, maybe in a dream.

But that was ridiculous. It was just weird because a man hadn't stood in this kitchen first thing in the morning in well over four years. Thomas and Duncan came over for dinner sometimes, but they never spent the night. So it was just weird because the last guy who did this was her dad, and she kind of hated him, even if it was wrong to hate dead parents.

She didn't think she made any noise, but Copeland looked over his shoulder at her. He hadn't shaved, and the dark stubble gave him an even more dangerous look. Not that he *was* dangerous, in the sense that someone shooting out her windows was dangerous.

But she felt…a strange kind of threatened when he looked at her like that. A fluttery kind of threatened, torn between running away and…

Well, she didn't want to consider the *and*.

He gestured at the coffeepot. "I can assure you, it's cop coffee, so it's not any good, but it'll get the job done."

She nodded, still feeling weird and shaken. So wordlessly she went over to the cabinet and got out her favorite mug and poured herself a very…thick semblance of coffee. She choked down the first sip on a grimace.

His mouth twitched. "You can always make your own."

She crossed to the fridge, rummaged around until she found cream. She checked the date. Only two days past expiration. Better than making her own pot of coffee. She dumped some in. It wasn't going to be enough, so she moved to the pantry, grabbed the bag of sugar and dumped some in.

"When are you going to go to the hospital?" he asked.

She could *feel* his eyes on her, but she was not about to look at him, even if she was surprised he was thinking about Vi. She'd choke down the sludge disguised as coffee and pretend like it was oh so normal to have this man in her kitchen. "It depends. You may be unaware, but babies don't let you know when they'll arrive. Even when you're induced."

The silence to that was incredibly uncomfortable, and she wasn't sure why.

"I'll drive you in when you're ready," he said, after the silence had stretched out. "Head into the station and handle some things. Then I'll drive you back. In the meantime, I'll help with the chores again."

It was the high-handed way he said all that, without *asking*. Without even *suggesting*. Just swept into her life and told her how things were going to be.

"I don't recall hiring a bodyguard."

"You'd do well to think about it."

With what money? she wanted to retort. But she didn't, because she had pride. Maybe too much, but better too much than too little. "Don't you have a job?"

"Guess what? Finding out who committed property damage and is making threats against a Bent County citizen *is* my job. Lucky you."

God, he was so grating. "But your job is not *my* chores. You don't—"

He interrupted her, gaze steely. "Don't say it, Audra."

"—have to."

He huffed out his own irritated breath. "Damn, you have a complex."

"Well, it's my complex to have. Maybe *you* have a *helping* complex."

He snorted. "Yeah, tell that to my ex-wife." Then he stiffened, his expression tensing. Clearly, he had not meant to let out that little tidbit.

Ex-wife.

So none of her business, but she stood still, tense herself, just…absorbing this new piece of personal information about him. She would never have claimed to know him. Literally the only thing she knew about his life before Bent was that he'd been a detective in Denver.

The end.

Ex-wife. He had an *ex*-wife. He'd been *married* when he seemed like such a loner. Maybe that was why he had an ex. *Ex*-wife.

But she wasn't Rosalie. Or Franny, for that matter. She didn't ask uncomfortable questions. She didn't poke into other people's private business. Even if she desperately wanted to know more.

Had to know more. "You were married," she said, instead of keeping her mouth shut like she *should*, like she normally would.

The stoic expression and tension in his shoulders didn't change. "Yeah."

"And divorced."

"That's usually what the *ex* means."

"I… Is that why you moved here?"

He lifted a shoulder. "Yes. No. Complicated."

She wanted a real answer, and knew she didn't have a right to one. "Right. Sorry. None of my business."

"You got any ex-husbands rolling around?"

She laughed in spite of herself. "No." She didn't know what possessed her. She knew she shouldn't say it. It had nothing to do with him, and it was ancient history, but it felt…fair, somehow, to let him into a piece of her not-so-great past. "I did date Xavier Stanley."

"That asshole? Damn, Audra." He shook his head, but he didn't seem so uncomfortable. He seemed almost faintly amused. "Have better standards."

"I do. Now. But in high school I was just thrilled someone asked me out. He wasn't as big of a jerk then, but he was working on it. Anyway, we all make mistakes."

He looked down at his mug, pushed off the counter he'd been leaning against. "Yeah, we do. We better get to work. I've got some calls to make later, when it's an appropriate time to be awake."

She nodded, agreeing with him, except…

What kind of mistakes had he made? What kind of mistakes led to an *ex*-wife and a downgrade in job status? It wasn't her *business*, but…she couldn't let it go.

She didn't know what divorce was like, because her father had preferred to keep two wives rather than let one go. Was Copeland the kind of man who would have done the same? She didn't want to think it of him, but…she had to know. Even if it was absolutely *none* of her business.

She had to know.

SHE DIDN'T FOLLOW him at first. Which was fine and dandy because Copeland didn't want those big blue eyes on him looking all…he didn't know. Certainly not sympathetic. Not that she should be.

Sure, he hadn't meant to mention Danielle. He usually didn't think about her or the life he'd left behind, but the past few days had...dredged stuff up, he could admit.

When Audra did finally follow him, she had a strange look about her. He couldn't quite read her expression or the way she was wringing her hands together.

"Copeland. You... With your wife. Ex-wife. You didn't... It wasn't..."

He stared at her, wondering what the hell she was getting at. Wondering why the hell she was harping on this. Wondering why the hell he was letting her.

"Spit it out, Audra."

"It's just..." She shook her head. "You won't get it. I know you won't. But my dad had this whole secret family. For years, he built a life with two different women, raised two different sets of children, and we never knew about each other until he died. And then it was such a mess. All because he didn't think about anyone but himself."

She was getting all worked up. He couldn't imagine going through that. His dad was just...one of the best men he'd ever known. His parents, their stability and goodness, were the foundation of his life, and the only reason everything back in Denver hadn't totally ended him.

But why was she bringing it up? She'd already done a tit for tat when she'd admitted to dating that prick Stanley. "What exactly are you asking me, Audra?"

"I don't know. I have to trust you, don't I? To stay here and allegedly protect me and all that. And I didn't really think about that on a personal level, because you're a police officer and Thomas trusts you and likes you and..."

"I didn't cheat on my wife," he ground out. Disgusted with himself and the situation and *her* for drawing this very private and none-of-her-business information out of him. He didn't *owe* it to her, any more than he needed her to trust him.

But he found he wanted her to know, whether he liked that want or not. "Quite the opposite." But that wasn't the whole story, was it? "Doesn't mean I wasn't a bad husband."

"I…"

"It also doesn't mean I'm a bad cop. In fact, probably the opposite. I'm not going to go start a second family, or even a first. So I don't see what it's going to do with anything."

"That isn't what I was getting at."

"Yeah, I know." God, he hated apologizing, but he was being a jerk, and he didn't have any reason to be. Maybe she was poking into his personal life, but…

He didn't know.

"Look, I'm sorry." He scowled at her. "Sore subject. Obviously."

"I…shouldn't have poked."

"No, you shouldn't have."

She huffed out a breath. "I just… I *know* it's none of my business. But I guess the idea of cheating and hurting people in a marriage is *my* sore spot, and I just want to be able to think of you as a good guy."

"Never said I was that."

"But you are."

She was so earnest sometimes. He didn't know what to do with it. "Then stop telling me not to help out, huh? Let me be Mr. Good Guy."

Her mouth curved, ever so slightly. "The good men I know aren't so grumpy."

"Even when you poke into their personal life?"

She pulled a face. "Not my usual MO. I leave that to Rosalie. But she's not here. So everything's out of whack."

He chuckled a little, imagining Audra being the yin to Rosalie's obnoxious yang. Maybe they did balance each other out, but Rosalie wasn't here and someone was harassing Audra and…

"Wait a second." He whirled around and she nearly stumbled back because she'd been moving with him toward the door. But with everything she'd said, it finally clicked.

"Second family. Death. Estates. Did your dad leave stuff to them? To you guys? A will? Contested? Ugly?"

"I…" She blinked. "Not ugly, I don't think. Mom was happy to sort of wash her hands of anything. Dad had transferred the ranch over to me before he died because he'd taken a job in agricultural sales. Well, that's what he'd claimed anyway. He didn't leave a will for the rest, so it was messy, but not ugly because we didn't fight for anything."

But death did funny things to people. Thinking they deserved things made once rational people act really irrationally.

"These other kids were okay with you getting all this?"

"I don't know what there's not to be okay about. I grew up here. This is my family's land. I…run this place and did before my dad died. I tried to reach out to them after I found out about them. I tried…to bridge a gap, but none of them wanted anything to do with me."

"I want names. And any legal documents about estates, possessions. Any legal document about the end of your father's life."

"Copeland, I really doubt some half siblings I've never met have some vendetta against me having the ranch. He's been dead for *four* years."

"I want names, Audra. It's the closest we've come to a lead, and I'm following the lead."

She had that stubborn look on her face. "It's a waste of time."

"My time to waste, sweetheart."

But he didn't think it was a waste at all.

Chapter Nine

Audra ended up having to put off doing her chores so she could list her half siblings who refused to talk to her for Copeland, and then give him the folder full of paperwork on her father's death. At least the paperwork that had been given to her. She suspected his other wife and kids might have some of their own that Audra had never seen.

She'd been fine with that. Maybe she loved her father, but she'd been happy for whatever he'd given to his other family to stay with them. Happy to wash her hands of whatever he hadn't given *them*.

Could one of her half siblings really be behind these strange, petty pranks? For what? And why after all this time? It just didn't make sense, and it frustrated her that Copeland wanted to go down this avenue because she couldn't see the *point*. Except digging into old, ugly wounds she didn't want dug up.

And she couldn't even be snippy about it, because she'd been poking into his divorce wounds, and she didn't even have a good reason.

Quite the opposite. That meant his wife had cheated on him, right? And that was probably why he was so grumpy and irritating. Or that was just who he'd always been. He said he hadn't been a good husband, but Audra refused to accept any kind of *excuse* for cheating. It was the most unnecessary way to hurt someone.

And none of this had anything to do with *her*. Once Copeland had everything he wanted, she went out to start her chores. She was behind now, and had to rush through or skip some things she'd have to come back to tomorrow, but if there was one thing she could use to justify rushing through or skipping, it was the prospect of meeting her new…

Well, Audra didn't know the exact specifics. Vi was her second cousin, but they always just called Magnolia her niece, and the new baby would be her nephew. And she'd be Aunt Audra to the both of them and whoever else came along.

If it made her a little wistful that marriage and her own kids seemed like such an improbability when she never got off the ranch and had *no* interest in anyone in the agricultural club, that was just life. She could throw herself into being an aunt.

She would.

But right now, she threw herself into ranch work. She checked fences, water, feed. It was a sunny day with a hint of spring warmth and that, along with an impending baby, put her in a good mood.

Until she stumbled, twisting her ankle and landing on her side. Surprised, shocked, she looked down at the ground and noted…something had been dug up behind the stables. And considering *she* hadn't been digging anything up…

She frowned at the overturned earth in a perfect rectangle. It was shallow, but it was long. Almost like a…

Grave.

Her heart gave a jerk and she looked around. The sky was blue, the scenery vast. She saw some cows out in the east pasture. The fence that separated her land from the Kirk Ranch.

But she was utterly alone out here. Her, the sky, the mountains. And only the vague hints that anyone would hear her if she screamed.

Everything that had once been a comfort now felt vaguely threatening.

You're being ridiculous. She got up off the cold ground, winced at the pain in her ankle. She didn't have time for a sprained ankle. Not that it was that bad. Just…she should probably stay off it for a bit and that wasn't happening.

She looked around again. No sign of anyone. Just this… shallow, rectangular hole. Maybe she was overreacting. Maybe Norman or someone from the Kirks had dug this for—for…something.

She shook her head. As much denial as she'd like to be in, with the ashes, the gravestone and the *shooting*…this was too much.

She pulled her phone out of her pocket. Instead of calling him, she just sent off a text.

I know you're busy, but I need you to come out to the stables.

In a few seconds, his response popped up. Asking for help? Are you dying?

She didn't reply to that as it felt a little too close to the overall vibe of the situation. She reminded herself that no one had tried to hurt her. That this was all silly scare tactics.

But *why*?

She waited, leaning her weight on her left leg over her right, until Copeland finally appeared over the rise, huddled into her father's coat. Still weird.

When he finally reached her, his expression was the usual stoic, not-quite-frown, definitely not a smile. Until he saw the hole. His eyes narrowed, his mouth firmed. Anger danced there.

"What the hell is that?"

"I don't know. It wasn't there yesterday, and it looks like…"

"Yeah, I know what it looks like." He pulled out his phone and began to take pictures. "Let me guess. You don't have any cameras out here?"

"On the entrance, but not here in the back." She would have gotten her back up about the way he was talking to her, but she was getting used to it. Starting to understand all that irritation was how he dealt with the situation, not really anything to do with her.

He swore under his breath, took a few more pictures. Then looked around, all while Audra stood still. She didn't want to move. Didn't want him seeing her limp. She had a feeling that would make his bad mood worse.

She wasn't foolish enough to think he cared about her, but she did think under all that bluster he *cared*. A sort of generic care that had driven him to be a cop, to solve crimes for a living. Whatever Thomas saw in him, under all the prickle, that made him consider him a friend.

"What should I do?"

"Leave it for now. I don't know that there's really much we can do with it, but I want to think it over before we mess with potential evidence. That doesn't mess anything up for you, does it?"

She shook her head. "No, it's fine as is." She'd need to stick a flag or something to mark it so she didn't trip and turn her *other* ankle, but she wasn't going to tell him that.

Especially with the way he was looking out at the horizon. There was an intensity in his gaze. Like he could just *look* and see whatever threats were out there.

She really hated thinking threats were out there.

"What else do you have to do? You shouldn't be out here alone."

"I've got a gun on me."

"You still shouldn't be out here alone. What else is there to do?"

She opened her mouth to tell him she could handle it, but then he'd get mad at her for saying he didn't need to help. Which was ironic, because it wasn't even about that now. She just didn't want him to see that she'd hurt herself.

Maybe she could walk on it without limping. Maybe she could...

"Why are you being weird?" he demanded. "What aren't you telling me?"

"Nothing. I was just thinking. I think that's about it for the day."

He looked up at the sky, then back at her. "You've worked yourself to the bone until dark every day I've been here."

"I planned a light day so I can go see the baby," she lied. Then she smiled at him. "You go on ahead. I'll catch up in a minute. I just have to lock up the stables."

He narrowed his eyes at her. She was usually a pretty good liar, but something about the man unnerved her. Always made her feel like he was going to see right through it.

"You've got dirt all over the side of your pants."

She looked down at them. "Oh. Well, you know. Ranching. Dirty work."

"You didn't have dirt all over your pants yesterday."

"Every day is different. The joys of ranching."

He shook his head. "It's a no-go, Audra. Spill. What happened?"

She blew out a frustrated breath. "I just stumbled on the hole. I'm fine." She took a step to prove it. She had to prove it. And winced and couldn't quite put her full weight on it. Cursed herself and the hole and whoever the hell was harassing her in the most obnoxious ways.

"You're limping."

"Just twisted my ankle a bit."

He bit off an oath. Just as she suspected. So irritated. So put out. "*Sorry* that someone is out to get me, and I can't seem to make that go away. You don't have to—"

He stepped toward her, and she stepped back instinctively, then let out a yelp when she put weight on the twisted ankle.

"Stand still," he ordered.

"What are you going to do?"

"What any sensible human being would do with someone who twisted their ankle. You could just lean on me and hop and hobble all the way back to the house, but that's dumb. I can carry you, so I'm going to carry you."

"You can't carry me."

"Is that a commentary on my strength or your stubbornness?"

"Neither. Copeland. It's—" But she didn't finish the sentence. He grabbed her, swept her legs out from under her, and then she was just…in his arms. And he began marching across the long expanse of yard.

It wasn't comfortable. It certainly wasn't *romantic*. But it did do something unfair and foreign to her insides. Scrambled them up. Because he *was* strong. She wasn't exactly a lightweight. Maybe she leaned toward skinny when she wasn't taking care of herself, but she was tall and sturdy.

He carried her like she was nothing. In her dad's coat that didn't smell like Dad anymore. He grumbled about her stubbornness the whole way, but he didn't put her down until he got her inside, where he dumped her on the couch. Except it wasn't exactly a *dumping*. He did it in a way that protected the injured ankle.

She couldn't find her voice, because that had been a whole...*situation* her heart and breathing hadn't recovered from.

He'd *carried* her. And now... Now, he was kneeling in front of her, unlacing her boot and tugging it off.

Gently.

Then he pulled off her sock. Her *sock*. His bare hands were on her ankle, and that was hardly sexual. It was hardly *anything*. Her ankle hurt when he pressed his fingers to it, but the rest didn't hurt. It skittered little sparks of something she would not name while he was doing it all the way up her leg, to tangle at the center of her like something very, *very* dangerous.

"It's swollen," he muttered. "You need to ice it, tape it up and stay off it."

The order cut through all the things happening inside of her body. She sat up a little straighter. "I can't stay off it."

"You can. You will. I know where the ice is. Got anything to wrap it with?"

"Yes, but—"

"Tell me where."

COPELAND PUT ice in the baggie he found, tossed it at her, demanded she elevate her ankle and put the ice on it. He didn't listen to her reply, just stomped to the upstairs hall closet she'd said the wrap was in.

He grumbled to himself as he pawed through the closet. She hadn't known exactly where it was, just that there was some in there. Figured.

It was a nightmare of packed shelves. Huge, and everything was in neat little rows, but the rows were of such disparate items it felt like a disorganized mess. He found all sorts of things. Old curling irons and other hair paraphernalia. Piles and piles of colorful towels of all sizes. Stacks of linens. A tub with the image of a cowboy on a horse full of loose pennies. A box of bullets. A medal of some kind. Two trophies that depicted a woman holding a gun.

He thought he was getting close when he found an old shoebox full of medicines with labels so faded they looked like they'd been here since the 90s. He pushed aside the box, paused when he came face-to-face with another box. This time of condoms.

Hell. He really did not need to think about that. He was about to give up, let her stomp around on her twisted ankle and her own stubbornness and call it a day, but as he was moving the medicine shoebox back into place, he noted a spool of wrap and grabbed it, muttering to himself.

Because now he was going to have to touch her again.

And he knew there were condoms in her closet.

No. She had two perfectly good hands. She could wrap her own ankle. She would be the first to tell him she could handle everything her damn self.

He marched down the stairs, propelled by that righteous certainty, until he made it to the couch. She held out her hand, that prim look on her face. Like a queen ordering a servant about. "I can do it."

He rolled his eyes, even though letting her do it had been his plan. It was an *ankle*. It wasn't the 1800s. He wasn't a man who got hot and bothered about an *ankle*.

He was damn well going to wrap her ankle. "Sit up."

"Copeland."

"Sit. Up."

She sighed heavily but sat up, moved her feet from their elevated position on the arm of the couch to the floor. He kneeled down. The pant leg of her jeans was still cuffed from when he'd checked out the status of her ankle.

He'd been in sports all through high school, so he knew how to handle an elastic bandage.

He kept telling himself that as he unwound the piece of fabric, then had to touch her again.

It's an ankle. Get a grip.

But no amount of self-flagellation seemed to make a difference. Touching her was like touching silk. This tough, do-it-all-herself ranch woman who had *shooting trophies* in her hall closet was soft and warm, and it really twisted something in him he'd long since refused to let be twisted.

Damn her.

As he wrapped her ankle, anger and frustration and something that felt far too close to fear not to put him in a bad mood, swirled inside of him until he'd certainly worked himself up into a lather.

He knew he should keep his mouth shut. He knew a lot of things. But temper won.

"Now, you're going to listen to me. I don't care how I-can-do-it and stubborn you want to be, you have to stay off this ankle. It's not a terrible sprain, but it's not going to heal if you're hobbling around."

"That's all well and good, but—"

"There are no *buts*. If you need help, you call in some help. I can handle a few things, but the Kirks *want* to help, so you're only being a stubborn idiot by refusing it. Well, sorry, pal. That's done."

He was still crouched in front of her, but he'd leaned forward, and now she did too, poking a finger into his chest.

"I didn't ask for you to be here. I didn't ask for your help or your opinion. I can handle myself."

"You're doing a piss poor job of it."

She dug the finger in deeper. "Screw you."

He put his hand over her wrist, pulled her finger out from drilling into his chest. "Yeah, right back at you."

He was too close, he realized in the silence that settled over them, fraught and angry. He held her wrist and they were eye-to-eye, practically nose-to-nose, in this odd little position.

Her cheeks were flushed with temper, and those blue eyes flashed with it. Her temper might have stoked his, but it wasn't just that. This close, just like last night, when they'd argued, it became something else.

Because neither leaned back. He didn't drop her arm and she didn't try to pull it away. They stayed right where they were. Too close and too annoyed by each other.

And too...something else. That incessant pull. A magnetic force all its own. A throb, an ache. He knew he shouldn't drop his gaze to her mouth, all twisted up into a scowl. And he knew *that* shouldn't make that ache deeper.

But it did.

She was just so damn pretty. Stubborn and obnoxious, and he was perverse enough to like exactly that. She didn't fall apart at...*anything*. And why that made him want to handle it all, he didn't have a clue.

But it was more than handling things because he wanted his hands on her and that was a line he absolutely had no business crossing.

Damn, he wanted to.

It would be an absolutely colossal mistake. There would be no defense, no crawling out from under it. If he touched his mouth to hers, everything imploded no matter how carefully he handled it.

And still, he was just a whisper away from doing it. Because no amount of rational thought seemed to break through this ridiculously tight magnetic pull that seemed to exist.

Then her phone rang, and they both jolted apart. Like caught, guilty teenagers.

For a moment, maybe just a second, they stared at each other, maybe in mutual shock. What *had* they been thinking?

But then she looked down and pulled the phone out of her pocket. He didn't miss the way her hand shook. The way she cleared her throat and licked her lips. And that was the problem.

He could deal with a little one-sided and inappropriate lust. It was a harder thing to do when the feeling was clearly mutual. *That* was going to lead to a very dangerous mistake.

"I-it's Thomas," she said, looking at the screen of her phone very, *very* intently. "Vi must have had the baby."

He gave a sharp nod, moved into a standing position, and tried to be very grateful about the perfect timing of the baby's arrival as Audra answered the phone.

Instead, he just felt edgy and irritable.

And it was all her fault.

Chapter Ten

Audra felt like she'd touched an electric fence. Her skin vibrated. And it wasn't a pleasant sensation.

Mostly because there was no *cure*. Except something very, very, very stupid.

And that wouldn't solve anything. Copeland Beckett was no knight in shining armor, even if he could look at her like that and turn all that frustration and anger into something else entirely.

She swiped the screen of her phone to answer the call before it went to voice mail, trying to pretend Copeland wasn't still closer than she wanted him to be.

And somehow not close enough at all.

"Hi, Thomas," she greeted, wincing at how shaky she sounded.

But Thomas must not have noticed, thank goodness.

"Baby's here. Fox Frederick Hart. Twenty-one inches. Eight pounds even. Pictures incoming. They're both doing great, and Vi said she's up for visitors whenever you want to come out."

It was the best distraction she could have hoped for. She could stop thinking about that low throb in the pit of her stomach, and the way Copeland's dark eyes hooked right into her and focus on new babies and family.

"Fox, oh, isn't that a perfect name? Magnolia and Fox. I

love it. I'm going to head out right now. Can I pick anything up on the way?"

"No. Between my parents and Vi's, we're drowning in just about anything we could need. We aren't going anywhere. I think she's going to video-call Franny. Too late in Italy to call Rosalie just yet, but we'll get there eventually. Vi just wants to see you, but no rush. Whenever you get here is just fine."

"I'm on my way. I can't wait. See you in a few." She clicked End. She didn't want to acknowledge Copeland, but she had to. Even if she didn't *want* a ride into town, she didn't want to fight with him over it. And worse, she didn't think she could drive very well with her ankle feeling the way it did.

He'd stood, taken a few steps back, but he regarded her with those intense dark eyes, and that stern expression made all the more *stern* by the stubble of the equally dark beard.

Just looking at him made her stomach do leaps and left her completely speechless.

"You need to stay off that foot," he said, which reminded her that words existed and so did her own will.

"I need to meet my honorary nephew."

"He'll still be around in a few days."

"I'm going to the hospital, Copeland. You can drive me, or I can drive myself. But I'm going." She even pushed off the couch to prove it. She put all her weight on her left foot and speared him with a stern look to rival his own.

He rolled his eyes. "Fine. Enjoy a bum ankle for weeks. What do I care? I'll drop you off like I said. I imagine you'll want to spend a few hours."

"Yes."

He nodded. "That'll give me time to head over to the station. Sit down and get your shoes on."

"I've got a present. It's upstairs." She gestured at the stairs.

"And I suppose you'd like me to get it?"

"I can—"

"Hell, Audra, just ask."

She didn't want to. She really, really hated asking for things, but hobbling up the stairs would be embarrassing and no doubt bad for the ankle. But she could leave it, give it to Vi later...

And that was too stubborn even for her. "Would you please get the present that's up on my dresser in my bedroom? It's wrapped with a bow, just sitting on the top."

"Did it kill you?"

"Not immediately, but maybe it will. A slow, silent death."

He chuckled, his eyes crinkling at the corners as he smiled and shook his head. It wasn't fair, that rare smile, that rare humor. Not at all fair that it had her insides getting all mushy. She much preferred the buzzing anger/attraction from fighting over anything that made her feel *soft* toward him.

He disappeared upstairs and she worked to get her boot on. She tested putting some weight on it. She could get by with a little limp, and not too, *too* much pain.

When he returned it was with the present, and a bottle of something in his hand. He tossed the present on the couch next to her, then disappeared into the kitchen. He returned with a glass of water, and two little pills she figured were ibuprofen in the other.

"Take those."

"Has anyone ever ordered you around?"

"Sure. I went through the police academy."

"And how much did you like it?"

He shrugged. "Part and parcel."

She scowled at him but took the pills because it was the sensible thing to do, even if she wouldn't mind being *asked*.

He didn't carry her to the car, which she was glad about.

Certainly not disappointed. But he helped her hobble over to it, carrying the present under his other arm.

The drive to the hospital was mostly silent. He turned the radio on at just enough volume to discourage speaking. Audra figured that was best. They'd probably just argue.

But in the silence, she found herself wondering about things she shouldn't. Like his ex-wife. Like what kind of husband he'd been. Like the fact he had been *very* uncomfortable the other night around Magnolia.

He pulled into a parking spot in the front of the hospital. "What lie are you going to hand out for why you're limping?" he asked as he shoved his car into Park.

"I'm not going to lie. I'm going to say I tripped and fell, which I did."

"Over a damn grave hole," he muttered.

"It wasn't deep enough to be a grave hole."

"Do you ever just let things go?"

"I let *everything* go. You're the one who doesn't let things go."

He just shook his head. "You got it from here?"

"Aren't you coming in?"

"Nah, going to head into the station. I've got too much to do. Just text when you're ready to head back."

She hesitated then, knowing that she'd do best to stop thinking about him, wondering about him, poking into his personal life. She'd do best to treat him like what he was. A detective on a case she was involved in. Beginning and end.

She couldn't manage it, because too many things added up, and now that she knew he had an ex-wife... She just had to know. "You don't...have a child, do you?"

He didn't look at her, stared straight ahead, his hands still on the steering wheel, but there was a tension in him. Still, his answer relieved some of hers. "No."

"It's just… You get a little…fidgety around Magnolia. When the topic of kids comes up, and now, you won't even come in and see the baby and… I just didn't know if it's something I should avoid. If—"

"I don't have a kid," he repeated. Stiffly this time, and with something in his eyes that she might have called *haunted* if she thought someone like Copeland had feelings.

Still, it was *something*. "But there's a sore spot there?" she pressed, not fully recognizing herself. She wasn't a presser. Though she did hate to accidentally tread on soft spots.

He sighed. It was the only sign he wasn't fully made of stone. "Sure. Sore spot. Yeah."

She couldn't imagine what it meant, but it made her heart hurt for him. "Okay. I'll be gentle around it."

He glared at her. "I'm a tough guy, Audra. You don't need to be gentle."

But that was just silly. "Everyone needs a little gentle, no matter how tough they are." She gave him a small smile. "I'll see you in a bit."

FIRST, COPELAND DROVE home and packed a bag of his things so he could stop borrowing Audra's dead dad's stuff. Then he drove to the police station. Grumbled some greetings before he made it to the detectives' office.

Where he would dive into work and forget about *gentle*.

Laurel was there but was clearly in the process of getting all her stuff together to leave. She glanced up at him.

"You been to the hospital yet?" she asked.

Copeland considered his answer. *Yes* wouldn't be a lie, but if she went in and talked to Hart, he'd be found out as a liar, and then they'd both demand to know why. "Not yet. I needed to get a few things done first."

She nodded, slipping a cross-body bag over her shoulder. "You still going to be MIA here tomorrow?"

"Unless another more pressing case comes up. I've got some leads on the Young shooting. Another little…weird happenstance. In fact, I'd like your take if you've got a few."

"Shoot."

He went over it with Laurel, wanting someone else's opinion on the matter. Because on the surface, this was all weird, petty scare tactics. But underneath it was all about *death*, and that was threatening. Not to mention the sheer amount of time and effort that was going into all these things.

"The father's second family is definitely something to look into," Laurel agreed. She'd taken a seat on the edge of the desk she shared with him. "But the way they're doing these things without leaving any clues, any evidence, it speaks to more local. Someone who knows the ins and outs of that ranch, of the system."

"She's got security, but it never seems to be where she needs it." He chewed over that. Someone who knew the ranch well. Could it connect to the Kirks? All the trouble they'd had last year? It didn't sit right, but he'd have to look in to it. "It just doesn't add up."

"My advice? Don't try to make things add up. People's motives don't have to. Keep following the evidence. Anything from the crematorium yet?"

"No, still wading through the red tape. Whoever runs the cemetery lives in California, and the maintenance guy I talked to didn't have any information. I've tried to figure out who made the stone, or engraved it, but I'm going to need records from the cemetery."

"I'll follow up on some of the phone calls tomorrow for you, see if it needs a woman's touch." She said that to irritate him like she always did, but he couldn't be ungrateful for the help. "Put Vicky on the records stuff. She's good at cutting through the red tape, and it's hard for you to do cozied up on the Young Ranch."

He snorted at the word *cozied*. "Yeah, it's a laugh a minute."

Laurel studied him, and he didn't like it. Especially when she changed the subject to something that made no sense.

"Did I ever tell you how I met my husband?"

"No, and you'll be shocked to hear this—I don't care." Not that he wasn't a *little* curious how the buttoned-up, professional, pain-in-his-ass Laurel had ended up with her bearded, tattooed, *wild*-looking husband.

She'd tell him anyway, but he kept up the image of not caring and went to his desk and pulled out his laptop. Booted it up and pretended like Laurel wasn't still standing there.

"It was a case. I was a newly minted detective, and Grady's half brother was suspected of murder. Clint's a mess, but he's no murderer."

He kept his gaze on the laptop. "Super."

"Grady was the opposite of me in every single way. Rival family even."

This time he did look at her. "Only in these backward places do you have rival families."

She grinned. "Bad news, Copeland, and I think you might already know this, though you'll pretend not to. You *love* this 'backward' place."

He scowled back down at his computer. Maybe Bent County wasn't so bad, but he wasn't about to admit it out loud.

"So Grady and I worked together to get to the bottom of it," she said, because Laurel never took a hint or even a direct no for an answer. "What do they call it? Forced proximity. One thing led to another, and here I am, all these years later. A husband and four kids under my belt."

"Good for you."

"It is. Really good. Because this job can be a black cloud, and it's good to have a reminder—whether it's family or friends—that there *is* good in the world."

He looked up at her again. "Do I look like I need some kind of weird pep talk?"

She met his gaze, both serious, instead of their usual ragging on each other. "Yeah, you do." She tapped her hand against the desk. "Email what you need done to Vicky. I'll talk to her if she has any questions. And visit Hart at the hospital. You're part of this community, whether you like it or not."

He didn't like it, he told himself, pulling up his inbox so he could write an email to Vicky. In fact, he hated it. Maybe he'd put in his two weeks. Head down south to sunshine and absolutely no ties. Yeah. That sounded good.

And even while he pretended, he knew he never would.

Chapter Eleven

The overjoyed parents were too besotted with their perfect, wonderful bundle to notice Audra limping. She got to sit and hold Fox in his perfect preciousness. She read an impatient and grumpy Magnolia a book for a little while to keep her occupied. She chatted with Thomas's parents, and Vi's dad, who carefully tiptoed around the subject of Audra's father, his cousin.

All in all, it was nice. It was refreshing to be in a happy environment, with family and friends and love and hope and excitement. For a little while, she relaxed and didn't think about being behind on chores or all the things happening to her that *seemed* harmless but had a whole lot of *death* in common.

She got sucked into *life*, and it felt wonderful.

Just when she was starting to consider texting Copeland because it was clear Vi was getting tired, even if she said she wanted everyone to stay, he appeared.

He brought flowers with a little balloon that said It's A Boy tucked into it. No doubt from the hospital gift shop, but it was still a sweet gesture. One that made Audra's heart mushy again.

"Do you want to hold him?" Thomas asked, angling the bundle toward Copeland.

Copeland stepped back as if Thomas was offering a grenade. "Nah, I like 'em a little sturdier. Congrats and all, though. I'm going to take Audra back, if that's alright."

Audra got to her feet, didn't wince. The ibuprofen *had* helped, and even if she hadn't elevated her ankle, she'd stayed mostly off it. She bent over the baby bundle, gave Fox's forehead a gentle kiss. She gave Thomas a hug, Vi a hug, and Mags a big squeeze. Exchanged goodbyes with all the happy grandparents, then followed Copeland out of the hospital room, high on family and love.

"Here," Copeland muttered, taking her arm so she could lean on him a little bit while she limped.

And that was nice too. She couldn't depend on it. She probably shouldn't even enjoy it. There was no one to lean on in this life except herself.

Which was the depressing pinprick to her bubble of happiness. Once in Copeland's car, it was another silent ride back. So silent, Audra actually dozed off in the passenger seat. She woke up, groggy and out of sorts, realizing only after a few blinks that the car wasn't moving.

They were parked. In front of her house. The world was dark around it, but lights shone on the porch and upstairs. He must have left them on since she knew she hadn't. He must have done it on purpose, with forethought to when they'd return.

Her heart ached. She wanted someone to do that sort of thing, someone to lean on, and yet she never let herself lean, so where did that get her?

Alone with no one to lean on.

But not disappointed. Not hurt. Just…drowning, apparently.

She shook her head. It was just this weird threat thing. It was messing with her equilibrium. Once it was solved, and Copeland was back where he belonged, she'd be back to normal again.

He was getting something out of the back of the car, so she pushed out of her seat. She limped toward the house, but

Copeland quickly caught up. He had a duffel on his shoulder but grabbed her arm. "What part of staying off your feet is difficult for you to comprehend?"

She decided to ignore him. "It was nice of you to bring flowers."

He shrugged. "That's what people do, I guess."

"But you were going to avoid it." They stepped into the cozy living room. She turned to look at him. "What changed your mind?"

"I wasn't going to avoid it. I just had some work to do first."

She opened her mouth to delve into that, then remembered she'd promised not to poke at his sore spots, so she just nodded.

"Hungry?" She moved for the fridge, realized she should have asked him to stop at the grocery store. The only thing she had to offer was eggs.

She pulled out the egg carton, glanced at him to ask him if he had any preference for how she prepared the eggs, but he was standing there, scowling, something angry and volatile pumping off him.

That sore spot, vibrating with pain. She desperately wanted to know what had caused it, how to soothe it. She wanted to know so much, but she'd promised…

"Fine. If it'll get you to stop looking at me like that, *fine*."

A little stung, she tried to argue with him, because she was *trying* to let it go. "I'm not looking—"

"It's nothing, but you're not going to let it go."

Completely offended now, she set down the eggs a little too hard. "I—"

"My ex-wife was pregnant when we got divorced."

That shut her up right quick, with a sharp ache of pain for him. No wonder kids and family were a sore spot. Because however this story turned out, he'd said he didn't have a child. And she could see the pain in his eyes even if he didn't want it there.

"The kid wasn't mine. She let me think it was though, for a while anyway. So, yeah, the whole my-friend-is-a-new-dad thing is a little weird and reminiscent of a terrible thing that happened a long time ago. The end."

She didn't breathe. It was…terrible. She knew he didn't want sympathy or thought he didn't. But she also knew, whether he realized it or not, he was saying this because *he* needed to. Because it was weighing on *him*, eating at *him*.

He'd stepped into a hospital room where he once thought he'd be in Thomas's spot, but instead he was just this…solitary outsider.

Even though she wasn't sure he'd welcome it, she moved over to him. Put her hand on his shoulder, rubbed her palm up and down in a hopefully comforting move. "Copeland, that's awful."

He didn't jerk away like she expected him to. He stood there, glaring at some point on the wall behind her. His breathing wasn't quite steady, and the anger and grief pumped off him. He'd no doubt bottled it up all evening, and now it needed to come out.

But when he spoke again, most of his anger had fizzled into a sad kind of bitterness. "You know what the worst part is? I would have stayed. I offered to stay. Be a dad, because the father was dead, and I'd loved him too. And after all that—cheating on me with my best friend, mourning him with me when he was killed, telling me she was pregnant with *my* kid—she still said no."

"That's…"

"It was a long time ago." He stepped away from her hand. "I don't know why I…" He shook his head. "We need to eat something, get some sleep."

"We'll do scrambled eggs and toast. Not exactly gourmet, but it's all I got." She limped over to the counter, tears burning in her eyes. He would *not* appreciate them, so she blinked them back as best she could as she scrambled the eggs, sliced some bread and tossed it in the toaster.

He got out plates. She was out of juice, and it was too late for coffee, so he filled glasses with ice water. They worked in easy silence as they got the meal ready and then sat at the table and ate it.

She managed two bites before she couldn't take it anymore. "Tell me the whole story, Copeland. I think you'll feel better."

He shook his head, merely pushing the eggs around on his plate. "There's no feeling better."

"Maybe. But bottling it up… Believe it or not, I get it. I'd rather never talk about a lot of things, but Rosalie always makes me. And it's usually better. It's like…you know, getting the toxins out. Have you ever talked to anyone about it?"

"My parents know everything."

"But have you ever…laid it all out? Told the whole story. Got it out of your system? The grief doesn't just disappear— how could it? But everything's magnified when you just hold it in. Until one day, it explodes." She mimed the explosion with her hands.

"You mean like dumping that all out on a near stranger."

"I think cohabitating has moved us up from stranger to at least some form of acquaintance. Maybe even friend. The kind of friend that lends an ear when someone needs it." She refused to look away, instead held his hurting gaze. "Like it or not, admit it or not, you need it."

THERE WAS JUST something about her. Against all his normal excuses and certainties, Audra dug under something.

She weakened that wall he'd built between himself and the past. He didn't *want* to go back there, but she made it sound like he had to.

Like he might actually survive if he did.

Copeland wanted to resist that pull. Resist this…connection. But she was just sitting there, looking at him, pretending like she knew how to make all this pain go away, and he was desperate enough to listen to her.

"We grew up together, Ethan and I. Became cops together. I went into the detective bureau. He went into SWAT. He liked the immediate danger. I liked the puzzle. I met Danielle while we were out one night, started dating her, got married. He gave me a hard time about tying myself down, but when we bought a house, he bought the one next door. I figured someday he'd settle down too, we'd raise our families next to each other. Our wives could be friends. It's hard being a cop's wife. Good to have community."

It still hurt, a deep, pounding pain that he thought he'd never escape. Those dreams he'd had for a future, and just how almost everyone he'd loved and trusted had made it impossible.

But he wasn't one of those guys who blamed everyone else. He'd had to look at himself clearly and honestly to make the decisions he had. And one of the honest truths he'd uncovered was that he maybe kind of deserved it.

"I loved being a detective once I made my way up the chain. I threw myself into cases. I wasn't home. The job became my life, and Danielle became someone…at home to handle everything. Ethan worked different hours than I did, so he helped her out. I can't be shocked she cheated. I can't begrudge her that." He'd worked very hard to believe it.

But Audra's words were hard, surprisingly hard from such a soft woman. "You can. You should. You got married. You made vows. The least she could have done if she wanted to break them was tell you that. Up front. And what about him? Your *friend*? He owed you more. Better."

Copeland shook his head. Maybe that wasn't altogether untrue, but… "It's complicated."

"I don't doubt it, Copeland. And no one's a mustache-twirling villain here, but the truth is pretty simple. Hard, but simple. They wanted the easy way out, and you don't get to blame that on yourself."

He let out a long breath. Wondering if he'd ever feel more like a stab-wound victim, always just barely surviving bleeding out.

It was easier to blame himself, because then he could live with it. If it was his fault, his mistakes, then he deserved it. And he handled that a lot better than thinking he didn't.

"So your wife and your best friend betrayed you. And they were *wrong*," Audra said, so firmly, like she knew, even though she'd never met Ethan or Danielle. Never known him as he'd been back then.

It was disorienting.

"She was pregnant. Was it his?" She asked it so matter-of-factly, but it didn't make him feel matter-of-fact. Nothing could.

"Before I knew she was pregnant, maybe even before she knew, Ethan was shot and killed in a hostage situation. It was rough. I thought it was odd how hard Danielle took it, but then I decided it was about…me. She was worried it could happen to me. It changed my perspective. I realized all the ways I'd been failing at being everything outside of a detective. Then she told me she was pregnant and I… I wanted that. A shot at that. The kind of family I'd had growing up. My parents are great. My childhood was great. I just thought, hey, I can make that happen. I could learn something from losing Ethan. It wouldn't have been in vain."

Sometimes, he wondered if that had been the worst part. That he'd wanted to make something good out of the bad and just gotten more and more bad in return.

"It lasted a few months. I went to appointments. We started planning a nursery. I thought…things were going to be okay. I was going to make up everything I'd screwed up. Then one night we got in a fight. I don't even remember about what. Something small, I'm sure, and she said she wished it was me that had died instead, at least then the baby's real father would be around."

Audra touched him then. Her hand over his fist. He hadn't realized he'd curled it on the table, but he could still see it in clear, perfect color. The anger, the bitterness, the *hate* on Danielle's face.

And then, the ensuing miserable guilt.

She'd apologized, but it had broken something. For both of them. And even when he'd offered to stay out of some kind of misplaced duty, she'd refused.

"She apologized, and after we'd calmed down, I offered to stay. Start over. But… She just wanted me out of her life. A fresh start. Her and her baby. The end."

And that had been that. She'd walked away, and there'd been no way to make her stay. No way to repair what she'd broken. Except to pretend like they'd broken it together. Pretend like the kid he never met didn't mean anything to him. Just…pretend, and pretend his way into being someone else.

"I tried to… I don't know. Keep working. Keep living. But I was someone else. I'd lost everything, even that…core of who I was. I couldn't stay there. I wasn't me anymore. So that's why I came here. To be someone else."

It sounded ridiculous when he said it out loud. So why had he? Why had he let Audra drag this out of him? It was so…

"I know how that feels," she said very quietly. So quietly, he had to lift his head, to make sure he wasn't dreaming she'd said those words.

She wasn't looking at him. She was frowning at the kitchen sink, but her hand was still over his. "To feel like two different people. Before and after, even if I didn't leave. Everything in my life is before my dad died, and after my dad died. And not in that sort of…grief way. In an angry way. That loss of something that wasn't right, wasn't fair. It's…sharp, so it just sits there. Bitterness. I don't like to be bitter. I don't like the way it…infects everything, and the people I love. So I liked it like that. Before. After. I could be someone else after."

Why should she understand? Why should she be the one to hold them accountable? Why should this unplanned forced proximity have led him *here*, talking about things he'd wanted to bury and leave behind?

Except he hadn't left anything behind. The past always clung to him. A layer of something he'd never been able to wash off. Weights that had stayed right there, his whole time here.

Until now. Somehow, she'd been right. Laying it all out—from start to finish—was a weird kind of exorcism. He'd always hate it. That betrayal would always be a part of him. The loss of a child that wasn't even his.

But…there was something about laying it all out to someone who hadn't been there, didn't know anyone, so stoutly saying what he'd always felt deep down, always tried to talk himself out of.

No matter what *he'd* done wrong, they had been wrong to hide it from him. Danielle had been wrong to let him think he was going to be a father. They had been cowards, and he wasn't perfect, God knew, but he'd always been honest.

"You know, I kept this secret from Rosalie for years. I mean, *years*. And I finally told her last year. I didn't want to tell her. I hated telling her, but I had to. And then, I felt better. To not have it anymore. To be able to tell her everything I felt. You just have to be able to let it go sometimes."

"What was the secret?"

She pulled her hand away from his, looked down at her plate, poked at what was left of her eggs. "Oh, I'd just sort of... Our parents sucked. Always. I was pretty aware of it, but Rosalie was younger. So I just...did a lot while we were growing up so she didn't know how little they cared about us. I made sure my parents paid attention to her, wished her happy birthday, got her presents—that kind of thing. I did things for her and gave credit to my parents. So, in a weird way, when we found out about my dad's second family, it hit her harder. Because she'd idolized him, but what she really idolized was the version of him that I'd created."

He could only stare at her. It was completely and utterly selfless. She hadn't done it for herself. Just for her sister, and even if it had backfired a little, she'd had the best of intentions. She even felt *guilt* over those best of intentions, like it was somehow her fault.

He had never met someone so bound and determined to hoard every responsibility for themselves, and he imagined she'd just been soldiering that weight her whole life. The weight of this ranch and her sister.

She wrinkled her nose. "I guess that doesn't do anything to deny the martyr claims." She got up, took their plates and crossed to the sink.

He grabbed the glasses and followed. He could say something nice. He actually found that he *wanted* to, but it was dangerous ground here. He recognized that enough to agree with her. "No, it sure doesn't."

She started rinsing off the plates. "I guess I am." She shrugged. "It is what it is. And now we've gone down those little memory-lane trips, gotten to know each other a bit, we can call each other friends now," she said, forcing some cheer into her voice. Then she looked at him and smiled.

Copeland didn't get involved. He didn't get wrapped up. He didn't vomit out his past at the drop of the hat. Whatever she turned him into, it wasn't *him*.

This wasn't exorcising anything. It was dragging it all up and tying her to it.

And he wanted her more than he could ever remember wanting anything. Especially when she laughed. Especially when she looked at him like she was just as irritated she wanted him as he was that he wanted her.

When she looked at him and *smiled* and said they were *friends*. When she'd done something he'd stopped everyone else in his life from doing.

She stood up for him. Pointed out the flawed thinking that he'd had a role in what two people he'd loved and trusted had done fully behind his back.

Oh, he knew his parents blamed Danielle, and even poor dead Ethan, for what they'd done. But he hadn't let them act on that, or say it to him. It had been easy to brush off any of their commentary as a parents' blind eye to their only child's flaws.

But Audra wasn't blind. He hadn't been exactly *nice* to her, even if he'd helped her. He didn't think she had any pie-in-the-sky ideas about who he was. And still, she'd seen everything he'd laid out for what it was.

Wrong.

He'd never had that. Hadn't *let* himself have it, and he wouldn't have even all these years later, but it had just… happened. *She* had just happened. And he didn't know anyone like her. Never had. She was damn confusing, was what she was. One minute all soft and self-sacrificing, the next hard and demanding and always…*always* carrying too many weights on her shoulders like she was the only one who could.

Her smile faded. She probably saw what was in his expression, but she stood her ground. He could walk away. He could—

But she stepped forward. She didn't shy away from meeting his gaze. She had to see the conflict there, between the things he shouldn't want and the things he did. And maybe he thought he saw the same things in her gaze. That was what gave him the permission.

Because if anyone deserved the things she wanted—even if she shouldn't—it was this woman right here.

So he kissed her. Just swooped down and pressed his mouth to hers, settled his hands on her hips and drew her in.

He kissed her until he forgot there was anything else in this world except the feel of her mouth against his.

She kissed him back. That impossible mix of sturdy and soft. Demanding and giving. And when she leaned against him, of her own volition, he felt like he'd won a war.

It wasn't wild so much as rooted. Tangled. It felt like being pulled under and into something he didn't understand, or maybe was afraid to. But the honeyed pleasure of the taste of her in his mouth coated any fear.

She wrapped her arms around his neck, leaned into him fully. He would have leaned right back, but something flickered in his peripheral vision. For a second, he thought maybe he was seeing stars, but it penetrated. How wrong it was. The flicker against the dark. He managed to get his mouth off hers, turned his head and…

"Audra. Out the window. Fire."

Chapter Twelve

Audra didn't understand the words at first. Her body was a riot of sensations and...fire.

Fire. Actual fire. All that heat, sizzle, fascinating intensity, drained out of her into a cold, icy fear as her eyes finally accepted what she was looking at.

Copeland had already started moving for the back door. His phone was to his ear and he was barking out orders to whomever he'd called.

She took a stumbling step forward, her twisted ankle forgotten until pain shot up her leg. She swore at herself, then limped another step toward the back door.

Copeland wrenched it open, but he turned to face her. His expression was all sharp lines, his words stern. The kind of order meant to be obeyed without question.

"Stay put."

She looked beyond him, to where the tool shed was engulfed in flames, shooting light and smoke up into the dark sky above. The shed was the closest outbuilding to the house. Luckily, it housed no animals, but it contained a lot of her yard tools and very little that could have just...spontaneously combusted.

He nudged her back. "Fire department is on their way. I need you to stay inside. I'm just going to look around the perimeter. You stay inside and lock the door."

She wasn't trying to be a pain. She wasn't trying to cause a problem. She was trying to understand, and she couldn't do it if she stayed inside. She couldn't comprehend… "Copeland. It's my place."

"I know it."

The conviction in his tone was strong enough, out-of-character enough, she moved her gaze from the fire to him. His dark eyes were intense, but it wasn't that impatience she was so used to. There was something more understanding there.

"You can't go limping around when someone was out there starting a fire on your property. You are the center of this Audra, like it or not. You have to protect yourself."

"What about you?"

He patted his hip, where he still had his gun from earlier. "It's my job, Audra. I'm damn good at it. I need you to let me do it, okay?"

She supposed it was that he was *almost* asking this time around that allowed her to nod.

He looked around the flames, the backyard. Cursed. "Look, stay off the foot if you can, but if you're looking for something to do, get yourself a gun. The front door is locked but I need you to lock this one behind me."

But locking him out sounded…bad and dangerous. For him. Her purse was right there on the counter, so she pulled her keychain out of it, then jerked open the junk drawer and retrieved a flashlight. She handed both to him, but he hesitated.

No time for that, she understood. She grabbed his hands and forced everything into them.

"Fine," he muttered. Then he was out the door, but she noted he waited.

Against her own instincts, she went ahead and flicked the

lock. Her brain was scrambled. Everything was...too much.
Everything was...

Burning. She blew out a breath. No. Just the shed. Un-
likely to spread anywhere else. But it was a threat or *something*, so Copeland was right to tell her to get a gun. She
limped out of the kitchen and over to the closet in the living
room. She kept most of her competition rifles in the base-
ment, but she kept a handgun on the main floor and one up
in her bedroom. Both locked away in safes, and not loaded,
but it always made her feel safer.

She shoved the tubs of winter hats and a few board games
to the side of the top shelf of the closet, typed in the code for
the safe, then drew the gun out. Cursing her painful ankle,
she went back to the kitchen, opened the junk draw and
pulled out the box of bullets shoved to the back. She loaded
the gun and then just stood there, looking out the window
at the flames.

It couldn't be a coincidence. It had to be another thing
being done *to* her. Why? Just *why*? These strange, dangerous
but petty things. Escalating in frequency. In danger. Nothing
overt. No evidence left behind. Just constant attacks on her.

No, not even her. The house, the truck, the shack.

It's my place.

Her place. Her ranch, and...everything that had happened
so far connected to *that*, didn't it? Not her, the *ranch*.

The power going out, the windows and her truck being
shot up, the shed on fire. These were attacks on the property—but not on anything that she needed to maintain the
cattle. Not on her actual person. These were petty things,
things meant to make her feel fear.

But they weren't hurting the *ranch*.

And if she wasn't here. If she was dead like whoever it

was had tried to make it look like with the cremains and the gravestone, the ranch wouldn't be hers.

But still, no one had tried to *kill* her. She could not make sense of it, but it felt like some kind of revelation. Not *her*. The land.

Someone wanted her afraid? Maybe someone thought she'd run away? It didn't fully make sense, but she thought there was the seed of something there.

The flames still shot up into the sky. If Copeland was anywhere around it, she couldn't see him. She didn't know if she should feel relief about that or fear. Could something have happened to him?

She swallowed down the fear. This was his job. He knew what he was doing. She had to trust that. Even as her heart hammered against her chest and she imagined about fifty million different terrible things befalling him out there in the dark.

But then she heard a siren in the distance, and eventually began to see flashing red lights, even though the fire truck hadn't appeared yet. She limped her way through the house to the front, only to remember there were boards there instead of windows now.

After a moment, the door jiggled, the knob turned. Terror clawed up her throat, but she reminded herself she'd given Copeland a *key*. Bad guys didn't have *keys*.

Copeland stepped into the dim entryway bringing cold air and the smell of burning in with him.

"Fire truck is here. They'll take care of it." He locked the door behind him before moving over to her. She watched as his eyes went to the gun, just a quick flick of his gaze. She didn't know what he thought of it, but there was *something* there in his expression she really couldn't read.

Didn't matter. What mattered was— "Copeland. I don't think this is about me. Not really."

"Hell, Audra." He stalked toward the kitchen.

She followed, trying not to wince at the pain. "No, listen to me. It's about the ranch. It's about…getting me off the ranch. So that's about me, I guess, but if someone wanted me dead, they could have done it quicker and easier before all this. All these scare tactics that haven't caused me any actual physical danger. They don't want *me*—dead or alive. They want the ranch. Or *something* about the ranch. If I'm dead, I don't own it, but they've only tried to make it look like I'm dead."

He didn't brush her off this time, though she wasn't sure he was actually listening to her either. He studied her, and there was no glimpse of the man who'd let her into the secrets of his painful past, no signs of the man who'd kissed her until her knees were jelly. This was *Detective Beckett*, and she was just a victim with information he wasn't sure he believed.

"Who would want your ranch?" he asked, in that same detached manner.

"I don't know." She really didn't. She didn't have the biggest or best spread. There was nothing particular or special about the Young Ranch. It was just an old family ranch like all the rest of them in Bent County.

But she knew she was on to something, because he didn't say anything. Didn't argue with her. He was considering, pulling at that thread. Or she thought he was.

Then he pulled a chair out from under the kitchen table and grabbed her arm. He nudged her into it, holding her weight so she didn't have to put any on her injured side.

"Stay off that damn ankle," he muttered. "And start thinking about who'd want to scare you off this place so they could have it for themselves."

THE FIRE WAS OUT, the firefighters and police that came were mostly dispersed now, but there was still one fire truck and one vehicle parked in Audra's front yard, and two men standing there talking too quietly for Copeland to hear from his place on the porch.

He was bundled up in his own coat *and* Audra's dad's coat because, hell, it was freezing out here. His only consolation was that he'd convinced Audra to stay inside. He'd suggested she make some coffee to offer, which wasn't exactly keeping off her ankle, but it was better than her standing out here.

One of the men was a firefighter Copeland thought was named Kline, if he remembered right, and the other man was Hawk Steele. Hawk was the fire inspector for Bent County. Lucky for Audra, he didn't live too far away. His place on the Hudson property with his wife and kids was just outside of Sunrise, so he'd appeared on the scene before the firefighters had gotten the blaze under control.

Copeland had worked with Hawk a handful of times, didn't have any negative impressions about the guy. He had a reputation for good work.

Which was a positive, because Copeland didn't need to know anything about fires to know that this one had been set on purpose.

Hawk probably wouldn't want to divulge much before he could do a more thorough examination in the daylight. Run tests on whatever he found, but Copeland hoped he'd be able to at least get confirmation of some things he was reasonably sure were true.

Both men approached the porch.

"The fire is fully out," Kline said. "No danger of it spreading. Steele here will go over with you what needs to be done to keep the scene from being contaminated for his investigation. Any questions or concerns, you've got my number."

"I'll want a copy of the report."

The firefighter nodded. "You'll both get it." He turned and headed for his truck, but Hawk took the stairs.

"I'm going to need to speak with Audra."

Copeland nodded, opened the door and gestured Hawk inside. "She's in the kitchen. You know Audra? One of those Bent-County my-cousin's-wife's-sister's-aunt's-stepmom-changed-my-diaper things?"

Hawk smiled. "I didn't grow up here, Beckett. But my wife works at Fool's Gold with Rosalie. I don't know Audra that well, but our paths have crossed."

"How much have you heard about what's been going on here?"

"Bits and pieces," Hawk confirmed. "Property damage. Death threats?"

"Sort of. I'll send you my reports on it, if it'll help your case."

"Can't hurt."

When they stepped into the kitchen, Audra had a full pot of coffee and some mugs out on the table, along with a small carton of cream and a little bowl of sugar.

"Hawk," she greeted and gestured at the table. "Coffee to warm you up? I made decaf, but I can put together a pot of—"

"Decaf would be fine," he replied easily. "Why don't we all sit down and talk?"

Audra nodded and moved for the table. She didn't limp, and Copeland knew it cost her. Just like he knew she *looked* calm and collected, but there were nerves in her eyes, if you knew where to look.

It was a little concerning that he knew exactly where that was. But that was a concern for a much different time.

She poured coffee for all of them, let everyone doctor their own mugs. Hawk took a sip. His nose and cheeks were red.

No doubt the warmth was welcome, but he didn't waste any time. He got right to it.

"I'm going to want to take a look again once I've got more light, maybe collect a few more samples, but I got the overall gist. It wasn't hidden or sneaky. Someone deliberately set that fire to your shed."

Audra swallowed as she nodded. "Yeah, that's about the only way I could have seen this going."

"I'm not fully familiar with the other trouble you've been having here, but Detective Beckett is going to share the case information with me, and I'll take it into consideration as I run some tests and see if we can figure out who did this."

Audra blew out a breath. "It'll be whoever is doing all the other things. And they haven't been too great at leaving us evidence to go on."

Hawk nodded. "It might be difficult, but fire's a bit more volatile. Harder to keep a distance from. We'll see what we can find, and I'll work closely with Detective Beckett since it seems likely it's related. That being said, and I hope you'll agree, Detective, Audra, you shouldn't stay here overnight. It'd be reckless to be alone out here at all, any time of day, until we know who's targeting you."

Audra opened her mouth, no doubt to argue because she was still the same infuriating woman, but before Copeland could tell her to knock it off, Hawk continued in his calm, even way.

"I know enough ranchers to understand it's a tall order to ask you to leave. You've got animals and a business to take care of, and I get that. But this is not a safe space until we know who's doing this. Fire is dangerous. Maybe they only meant to burn down that shed, but it was the closest structure to the house. Had the weather been dry, things could have ended up much worse. Just because no one's specifically tried to hurt *you*, doesn't mean you won't find yourself in the crosswind."

When Audra looked at Copeland, the pleading in her eyes about took him out, but he wouldn't relent. Couldn't when her safety was on the line. "He's right. You know he's right. You've been lucky so far."

"Lucky," she said disgustedly, pushing away from the table, coffee mostly untouched.

Hawk rose as well. "I'm going to head into the office, handle a few things, then I'll stop by once it's light. I'll keep you both updated."

Copeland watched as Audra turned to Hawk, plastered on that fake smile. "Thank you," she said, sounding like she meant it.

Copeland knew she didn't.

"Stay safe, Audra. Beckett? I'll be in touch." With that, Hawk nodded at both of them and let himself out.

For a moment, the kitchen was fully silent. Audra stood by the sink, brooding out the window. Copeland sat at the table watching her.

He could probably read her mind. She was trying to figure out how to convince him she should stay. Which was *stupid*, but worse than her stupidity was his. Because he was trying to rationalize it to himself.

If he stayed with her, she'd be safe. He'd protect her. He'd been here since the shooting, and nothing had touched her, even if it had touched the outside.

But someone had started that fire while he'd been *right* here. "If you're right, and this ties to the land and not *you*, then removing yourself from the land makes you *safe*."

"And leaves my home, my life, my *livelihood* unprotected."

"But you'll be *alive*, Audra."

Her shoulders slumped at that. "This place has been mine—my responsibility—since… God, I don't even know. It feels like always, and you're asking me to abandon it."

"I'm real sorry about that, but nothing is yours if you wind up dead. And Hawk is right. Maybe no one is after hurting you, but these things they're doing aren't benign. Shooting and fires. It's dangerous to be around, even if you're not meant to be the main target." He wasn't getting through to her, so he had to be strategic. "Franny will be back eventually. Are you going to let her stay here with all this going on?"

She glared at him. "You know just what buttons to push, don't you?"

"You said it yourself, right? We're friends. Friends know stuff."

Her glare didn't change. "*Friends* don't kiss like that," she muttered.

He could handle that reintroduction a lot of ways, but he wanted to see some of that horrible tension in her expression dissipate. So he went for light. "How do they kiss then?"

"They *don't*."

"Oh. Bummer."

The sound she made was *almost* a laugh, and that eased the pain in his chest a lot more than it should. But it didn't last. The weights, the worry, the hurt all came back. Settled in her shoulders, her expression.

She inhaled, and it shook. The vulnerability in the sound unnerved him, but also prompted him to move toward her, with some ridiculous urge to comfort, to fix.

He got a hold of himself before he touched her. He had to get a better grip on his reaction to her. The kiss hadn't helped, but he had to be stronger than some little kiss.

Little. Ha.

She turned to look at him then, tears swimming in her eyes making them an unearthly shade of blue. "I can't leave. Maybe you can't understand. But I can't leave this place. It'd be like leaving my soul behind. I'm not trying to be reckless or foolish. I wouldn't know how to be reckless if I tried. I've never had the time to be foolish. Leaving isn't an option for me, Copeland. I have to be here. I have to face this. I *have* to."

He studied her. Yeah, it was the martyr complex talking, but there was something deeper at the root of it. Something deeper than her desperate need not to put anything on anyone else's shoulders. She'd clearly been doing that since she was a kid. He didn't understand what kind of awful parents could instill that on their child, but what impressed him was that Audra hadn't let it make her bitter. Oh, she was a mess of issues, but she wasn't angry or bitter. Her kindness seemed inexhaustible. Her concern for others admirable…and contemptible when she let it supersede reason.

She needed someone to take care of her. To take some of those weights. No one could change her into someone who didn't take on too much, but she needed someone to share the load. Whether she liked it or not.

Not that it was going to be *him*. Not that it was any of his business how many weights she carried. That was her business. Her deal.

But he wasn't about to let her wind up dead in the process. Just because she loved this place like some people loved their children. Just because he couldn't bring himself to demand she leave when she had tears in her eyes and pleas in her voice.

"Fine."

Her entire posture relaxed. She even reached out to touch him, just a gentle brush of her hand against his arm. "Thank you, Copeland, for understanding. It means—"

"Don't thank me just yet. There's a stipulation."

Wariness crept into her expression, but she nodded, chin high. "Alright."

"You don't leave my sight. Twenty-four seven. You're somewhere? So am I."

Chapter Thirteen

Audra didn't respond at first. Mostly because far too many reactions to that *stipulation* rattled through her. Anger. Frustration. A bone-deep weariness that made her just want to sink to the ground and give up. Luckily, she was used to that feeling. She'd been fighting it for years now.

What she didn't know how to fight was the other emotions battling for space inside her.

Relief. Pleasure. Copeland would be by her side and that meant—

Nothing. It means nothing.

"Isn't that what we've been doing?" she asked, trying to sound casual. Trying to fight away all the *reactions* and just deal.

"No, I left you alone yesterday. That's when you tripped and hurt yourself. I left you alone at the hospital. I'm not being metaphorical. I'm being literal. Twenty-four seven or the deal's off."

That did nothing to ease the mix of emotions. He couldn't possibly do that, and she shouldn't want him to, but she kind of did.

She'd been denying her wants her whole life, so why stop now? She turned to face him, taking a deep breath meant to center, calm. She was used to dealing with Rosalie's ridiculous stubbornness. She could deal with his. She fixed him with the same older-and-more-with-it-sister glare she used on Rosalie.

"Copeland. You cannot be by my side twenty-four seven. You have a job, for starters. Not to mention all the *private* parts of a person's day."

He shrugged. "I'll figure it out. Now, let's get some sleep. It's been a long day. *Days*."

He was starting to poke at her temper. *I'll* figure it out, like she didn't have a say, when all she had were says. "You're not in charge of me."

"The hell with that," he retorted, without much heat, but a lot of conviction. "Someone ought to be. So while we're at it, you're going to have to tell Rosalie. Maybe you've got a few days, because she's so far away, but this is going to get back to her. Too many people know. Too many things have happened. You really want her catching wind of this from someone else?"

It was awful. Both prospects. Really awful because he was right. Hawk would no doubt mention something to his wife, and while Anna wasn't going to call up Rosalie on her honeymoon, there was just too much of a chance that it all got back to Rosalie sooner rather than later.

"Are you trying to make me cry?" she demanded, because she'd just gotten a handle on it, and now he was making it worse.

"No, and I'd really prefer it if you didn't."

She managed a watery laugh at that, blinked back the tears. "Yeah, I'd prefer that too."

"Come on," he muttered. He moved to her side, wrapped an arm around her so she'd lean on him more than put weight on her ankle. They walked like that in silence to the stairs. She tried to reach for the railing, but Copeland stopped her.

"You've got to give that ankle a break."

"You're not going to carry me again."

"You keep being so very wrong." And then, just like last time, he picked her up before she even had a chance to talk him out of it. Just an arm under her shoulders, another under her knees, and easy as you please, just up the stairs. Like she didn't weigh a thing when she most decidedly did.

He didn't stop there. He walked her all the way to her room. Then he very carefully set her on her feet and crossed over to flip on the lights. He surveyed it with those cool, detached cop eyes.

"Decent-sized bed," he commented. "Going to share it or am I sleeping on the floor?"

She gaped at him. Her mouth hanging open like a fish. "What?"

"Twenty. Four. Seven. I'm sleeping in this room with you." He patted his side. "Armed."

"I have a gun up here."

"Great. Two's better than one."

"Copeland." She knew there should be a reasonable spate of refusals to bring up, to get through to him, but all her brain seemed to come up with was: *what*?

"You're going to have to save us both time and energy and stop trying to argue. This is the deal struck."

His deal. *His* decision. As if her life was his to determine, when she'd been determining *everything* for her entire adult life, if not more.

It was his *job*, sure, and at the end of the day, as ridiculous as he was being, she knew she needed help. She knew whatever was going on was beyond what she knew how to handle or stop.

But she hardly thought that extended to sharing a room, to losing all her privacy and agency. She could tell him all that, but it wouldn't change anything. If there was anything the past few days had taught her, it was that there was no getting through to him, no winning this. He'd find a way. He had every single time, no matter her objections.

It infuriated her. She usually got around *everyone* with a sweet smile and doing what she wanted anyway. She usually convinced everyone she was so fine, so with it, so...*good* that she didn't need overbearing determinations.

Why was he different?

She went into the closet, pulled out the spare pillow, some clean sheets, perhaps a little unreasonably angry at him for being that different. She tossed everything on the ground, spurred on by fury and, if she was being honest with herself, maybe a little panic that someone had finally gotten through. "There. Enjoy."

She went back to the closet, grabbed some pajamas. Then tried to stride out the bedroom door, but he was right there. Right behind her the short walk across the hall.

She turned to scowl at him in front of the bathroom door. She gestured at it. "Just the bathroom, warden. I need a shower."

"I said you're not out of my sight. I'll amend that to give you private bathroom privileges, but that's it."

Bathroom privileges? How was he possibly serious? She fisted her hands on her hips. "Oh, well since I'm your prisoner did you want to handcuff me while you're at it? Maybe shower together so I'm never out of sight?"

He studied her, something about the way his eyes changed reminding her of when he'd kissed her. Her cheeks reddened. Because that was *not* what she'd meant, but the image...

Jeez, she needed to get a grip. So she turned on a heel and jerked the bathroom door open. She closed it behind her, not with a *slam*, but with a firm *snap*.

She flicked back the shower curtain, wrenched the water

on hot, then paused because…it was so *weird* that he was right outside the door, and she was going to take off all her clothes.

And if she called it weird, she wouldn't have to acknowledge that there was something else fluttering through her as she got undressed and stepped into the hot spray. Like the idea of *sharing* a shower. Or that kiss they'd shared. Or mixing it all up into one very inappropriate fantasy.

Yes, it is totally normal to fantasize about sex with a bossy, overbearing detective who is only here because your life is falling apart.

She wanted to groan, maybe beat her head against the wall a few times. Instead she washed up, got out of the shower, dried off and dressed, and then decided she'd handle the rest of the night by not speaking, not thinking, not worrying.

He could sleep on the floor. She'd sleep on her bed. And that was that.

Determined, recalibrated, she gathered up her dirty clothes and opened the door to move out into the hallway.

Copeland was leaning against the wall, looking at his phone. He lifted his gaze when she came out. His eyes moved over her. Not exactly a detached-cop look. No, there was the flicker of *something* in their dark depths.

She could convince herself the kiss was a mistake for a lot of reasons, but it was hard to remember those reasons when she was faced with the fact that whatever she felt about him, whatever reactions she had to him, she wasn't alone. He wasn't immune to her.

"I'm going to run through myself," he said. "You can head into your bedroom, but you stay there. We're leaving both doors open."

She wanted to have a snarky retort, but she just limped into her room, dropped the dirty clothes in her hamper, turned off the light. She crawled into bed. Her body was fully and wholly exhausted. Her ankle throbbed, so she took the bottle of ibuprofen out of her nightstand and took two with the water from the water bottle she kept next to her bed.

Then she flopped back on her pillow knowing that no matter how exhausted she was, everything plaguing her would keep her awake. And not just because Copeland was currently in her shower. Naked, no doubt. With the door open. She could hear it running. She could hear the occasional creak of his weight shifting the old house.

She squeezed her eyes shut and tried to fight off that potential image. Didn't she have bigger problems than an unfortunate and untimely attraction to a man who…

That was the trouble. She wanted him to be like he seemed. Cold and abrupt and cocky. And he was all those things when he wanted to be, but it was clearly an armor put on after a really awful time in his life.

He was here because he wanted to help. No doubt that was why he was in law enforcement. But she also knew, somewhere along the line, whether either of them admitted it to themselves, it had become at least a *little* more. And she didn't just mean the kissing.

He returned, but didn't flip on the light. She heard him move, the sheets rustle as he settled himself into his makeshift bed.

On the cold, hard floor. After everything he'd done to help her. She didn't *want* to feel guilty. It made her really mad that she felt guilty, because he didn't *have* to sleep on her floor, he didn't *have* to take on this responsibility.

She knew that was rich coming from her.

"I can't sleep with you lying on the floor," she muttered, staring at the ceiling in irritation.

"So trade with me."

"I'm not *that* big of a martyr," she replied, though she was beginning to wonder.

"Sure about that?"

Frustrated with him as much as herself, she sat up, leaned over the end of the bed to peer down at him. It was shadowy dark, but she could make out the lump of him lying on the hard, cold floor. She'd never be able to sleep knowing it.

"This isn't an invitation."

She couldn't see his eyes in the dark, but somehow she could feel his gaze all the same. "What isn't?"

"It's a big enough bed to share. If you can stay on your side."

Maybe she expected him to put up a *little* bit of a fight, but he *wasn't* a martyr. He immediately moved. He tossed the pillow onto the side of the bed she wasn't on, then she felt the weight of the mattress dip.

Why had she thought this would make it easier to sleep? Sure, guilt wasn't eating at her now, but everything else was. How close he was. How odd it was to feel the weight of someone else in her bed. The smell of her shampoo that he must have used mixed with whatever made Copeland... Copeland.

How had she gotten here, and how was she ever going to explain it all to her family when they returned?

Natalie thought she was sleeping with Copeland, and now she was in the most literal way possible. Rosalie would be furious she'd kept so much to herself. Franny would be hurt, because she could visit her parents anytime, so Audra really should have told her, let her come home.

And now she probably had to tell them both before she wanted to, just so they didn't hear some small-town-gossip version of everything.

Just the thought had the tears returning. She didn't know how to make it okay. How to make Rosalie not worry. How to keep Rosalie from ending her honeymoon early, or Franny rushing home. They wouldn't want her to handle it alone and they *should*.

The guilt of it was too much. This was *her* ranch, *her* problem. She wiped one of her now wet cheeks against the pillowcase. She breathed carefully through her mouth as the tears streamed down her face. She wouldn't let him know she was crying, this man who was stubbornly and platonically sharing her bed. She wouldn't…

"This isn't an invitation either," he muttered, drawing her close, then rolling her over so that she was tucked into his warm, hard chest. He ran a palm down her hair, brushed tears off her cheeks, and held her while she cried.

And because he did, she let it out. Sobbed out the whole awful ordeal. Just like what she'd said to him about telling her the whole story about his ex-wife. It was releasing toxins or *something*. She hated it, but at least it served a purpose.

She didn't like to cry on Rosalie's shoulder, or Franny's, or Vi's. Or Natalie's or *anyone's*. It made her feel weak and like she'd failed.

But this wasn't so bad.

COPELAND WOKE UP to sunlight streaming on his face, and a warm body moving next to his. For a moment, he instinctually held on. It was nice. It was…

His eyes popped open. He would have shoved into a sitting position, but he was met by blue eyes fixed on his face.

God, she was pretty. He didn't know how she could give off the aura of slim, delicate spring flowers knowing how strong, sturdy and determined she was. He knew she could handle anything and had, but he wanted to erect full fortresses to keep her safe.

He went from half-asleep to alert in a second, realizing

he had one arm under her shoulder, and she was resting her hand at his inner elbow. Like maybe they'd fallen asleep, wrapped up together, after she'd cried herself empty.

He should get up. Leave this warm cocoon of...*something*. He'd comforted her while she cried, and that was it. Friendly. Helpful. He was hardly going to use an emotional breakdown as a kind of catalyst for...whatever this moment seemed to demand.

But *she* didn't get up. She didn't scoot away. They were so close their noses were almost touching. And neither jumped up to move. Neither looked away.

He knew he should do something to stop this, but she was just so soft and warm. So damn beautiful it *hurt*. Something was beating through him. Heavy, important, mixing with desire and the hazy notion that this wasn't at all wrong.

It was, instead, exactly right.

She moved closer, close enough her body brushed his. Her mouth was just a whisper away. Her blue gaze never left his face.

He could close that little distance between them. He could kiss her, touch her. He could calm this thudding, needy conflict inside of him.

He could extricate himself. Slip out of bed. Pretend this wasn't happening.

But he waited, watching her.

Until she pressed her mouth to his. Sweetly and gently. Her hand coming up to trace his jaw, then raking through his hair. She was a descent into soft, honeyed perfection.

"Just so we're clear," she said against his mouth. "This *is* an invitation."

"Good, because I'm taking it." He rolled her under him, gratified when she made a little sigh of pleasure beneath him. When she met every kiss, every touch, every whisper with one of her own. And it released all that had tied so tight, because he'd wanted this for days now. Just this. Just her.

Sex had been a game since his divorce. Fun. Spontaneous. And very, *very* superficial. Something to do, something to prove to himself that even if he kind of sucked in the whole being-a-human department, he still *was* one.

There was nothing superficial about the way her skin felt, the way she moved under him, the way she kissed him. That was all a heavy, complicated braid of emotion, responsibility, want and something deeper than he had the words for.

It wasn't just sex, certainly wasn't a game. And he could try to convince himself of either of those things, but she already had too much weight in his heart for him to manage.

Being tangled up in her was a privilege and a hope. A tangled, changing dance. As pleasure throbbed, flowed and released in shuddering tandem that took both of them under in the early morning light.

He tucked her close and closed his eyes, and for a moment just breathed. There was so much to do, to handle. This was a distraction that wasn't right when danger lurked.

But, damn, it felt right.

"I guess you've got chores you're late for now," he said when he trusted his voice not to sound heavy with all the emotions waging war inside of him.

She made a contented noise, low in her throat. "I might have finally found something worth being late to chores for."

He should be distancing himself, but instead he pulled her in tighter, settled his face between her jaw and shoulder. Inhaled the faint, flowery scent of her skin that came from the soap she used in the shower last night, and it settled through him. Calm. Warm. Right. "I can make you even later."

"No, you can't and that's *not* a challenge."

He made a considering sound, pressed his mouth to the

underside of her jaw. She shoved at him, but with a laugh and with a lightness in her whole body he hadn't seen this whole time.

It was a heady feeling to be the one that got to take some of the weight off Audra Young's shoulders. Dangerously heady, and maybe he would have given himself a stern talking-to about that, but he heard the chime of a doorbell ring through the house, and they both stilled.

"Expecting someone?" he asked casually, trying to remind himself that people who shot out windows and set fires didn't *ring the bell*, so he wouldn't go tearing downstairs, gun in hand.

"No." She hopped out of bed, and he got one tantalizing glimpse of everything before she tugged on a hideous, fluffy robe. "It's probably Natalie." She sighed, weight seeming to pile back on her shoulders. "She probably heard about the fire. I'll be right back."

"Audra, wait—"

But she was already out the door. He cursed under his breath as he got out of the bed. It probably *was* Natalie, but she didn't know that for sure, and with everything that was going on, she had to be more careful.

He couldn't find his shirt, but he wasn't about to let her go downstairs on her own, even if was just Natalie. Twenty-four seven meant twenty-four seven whether she liked it or not, and sex certainly didn't change that. He pulled on his pants as he walked, then jogged down the stairs.

She had the door open, and he could hear her even though he couldn't see who was on the other side yet.

"Oh. Hello. Are you looking for Copeland?"

"Yes." Laurel's voice. "And you. We've gotten a few small breaks in tracking the cremains. I was on my way out to Sunrise for a different case and thought I'd stop by and catch you two up."

"Oh. Okay. Well, come on in." Audra moved out of the way and Laurel stepped in. She glanced around the room in a quick, cop sweep. She spotted Copeland at the bottom of the stairs in nothing but his unbuttoned jeans. Her eyebrows immediately raised.

"I—I'll make some coffee," Audra offered, a little too brightly. "We'll talk in the kitchen." Her cheeks were bright red, but she moved with just the hint of a limp, toward the kitchen, in her bathrobe.

Laurel followed Audra, but her gaze stayed on Copeland. He couldn't quite read it. Not contempt. Definitely not approval. Something more appraising.

"Nice tattoo," Laurel said under her breath as she passed him.

Cursing, Copeland went upstairs to find his shirt.

Chapter Fourteen

Audra wasn't sure how her life had spiraled so far out of control. Sleeping with Copeland was one thing. The kiss before the fire had sort of made *more* feel like an inevitability, and even now she couldn't regret it.

She'd been in long-term relationships before and nothing had ever felt like that. It wasn't just the physical part, though—*wow*. It wasn't that she'd felt like she'd uncovered something, discovering the coin-size tattoo on the front of his shoulder, in the shape of a police badge. It was that it had been *more* than all of that.

More than her usual trying to make a relationship last, work, be the *end*. It wasn't about relationships at all. It had just been about waking up to him holding on to her, knowing that he was…a good man. And she'd wanted some piece of that.

The weight of it had been important, somehow. And it was one thing to try to work through all *that*, but for his *coworker* to show up… To see it. That was something else entirely, even if Detective Delaney-Carson was being very nice and pretending like she didn't know what was going on.

Audra stood at the coffee maker, discarding the remnants of last night's decaf and getting it set up to brew. Copeland reappeared with his shirt on before she finished.

He gruffly ordered her to sit down. Audra didn't miss the

considering gaze the detective gave Copeland, but she pretended she did. She sat, not bothering to tell Copeland her ankle was feeling better. He'd just argue with her.

"Sorry to interrupt your morning," Laurel said, giving Copeland a pointed look when he put a mug of coffee in front of her. She moved her gaze to Audra, and it was kind. "But all the ranchers I know are up at the crack of dawn and I have a meeting in Sunrise in an hour. I figured I'd stop by instead of having you two come out to the station, because we've got something of a lead."

"You could have called," Copeland muttered. He put a full mug, with a dash of cream, like she always took it, right in front of Audra.

"I did," Laurel replied. "Left you a message. I guess *you* could have checked your phone."

Copeland's gaze flicked to Audra, and she couldn't stop the heat from creeping into her cheeks, because obviously they had been *busy* when that call came in.

"What kind of lead?" Copeland said, his attention back on Laurel. He grabbed his own mug of black coffee and sat down in the chair between them.

"We still don't have any suspects, but we've managed to trace the payment to the funeral home that made the arrangements for the cremains. Unfortunately, the payment was made from a fake identity, but the money still had to come from somewhere. We don't have an answer to that just yet, but we do know the payment came from Florida, and we're working on the theory that the person, regardless of fake identity, is somewhere in Florida. Or was. Florida feels like where a lot of this is originating from, even if someone is here now doing these things."

Florida. Audra heard a strange buzzing in her ears, like she'd been transported somewhere else. Florida.

A coincidence. It had to be a coincidence. Florida was a big state. It wasn't... Why *would* it be?

But when she came back into herself, certain it was a weird coincidence, Copeland was frowning at her.

"Do you have any connections to Florida, Audra?" Laurel asked.

But Audra couldn't look away from Copeland.

"You know someone in Florida who might be out to get you?" he asked grimly.

She shook her head. "No, I don't know anyone who's out to get me." Not here. Not anywhere. Why *would* she?

He narrowed his eyes. "Audra, who do you know in Florida?"

She managed to find her voice, though it was a hard-won thing. She couldn't look at Copeland as she spoke, so she looked at some vague point on the wall. "Only one person. My mother." She tried to smile. "Obviously my *mother* doesn't have anything to do with this."

But Laurel and Copeland exchanged a look that said "not so obviously."

"My mother doesn't want the ranch," she continued quickly. "Or to hurt me. She'd have to care about either. She left the minute she could. She wanted *nothing* to do with this place once she found out about Dad's other family. She wanted nothing to do with..." Me. Us.

"And before that?"

She looked at Copeland helplessly, because this wasn't a lead. It couldn't be. "Before what?"

"Before she found out about the other family. Before his death. What did she feel about the ranch before that? Because you guys were here, so she had to have some feelings. Why did she leave?"

Audra couldn't find any words. Maybe because as impossible as it *seemed*, she… She knew how angry her mother had been. Understandably. *Rightfully.* But it had turned against everyone, and for so many reasons, the experience with her father was easier to deal with. He'd lied, cheated, betrayed. Died. It was easy for Audra to hate him and be done with it.

Everything she felt about her mother was a jumble. She couldn't blame Mom's bitterness on anyone but Dad. Couldn't blame Mom for leaving her and Rosalie to clean up the mess. He was their father, their blood. Not hers. To her, Dad was just a mistake she'd made for too many years.

Maybe Audra had thought…a good mother stayed for her kids, supported her kids, regardless of the father, but she also couldn't pretend to know the level of betrayal from the man you were married to having a whole other family he left things to.

So she tried not to blame Mom too much. She tried not to expect anything out of her either. She tried to be neutral. Maybe she'd been leaning closer to anger when Mom had refused to come to Rosalie's wedding, but Audra didn't think Mom knew that. Or cared.

And none of this was…right. "She left because she hated this place," Audra told Copeland. "She wouldn't come back just to…mess with me. She doesn't care about anything here. Florida is a coincidence. It has to be."

Laurel and Copeland shared a look. Not disbelieving exactly, but the kind of look that said they were going to look in to it one way or another.

Audra knew she was just going to have to deal with it.

COPELAND WALKED LAUREL out to her car. They paused at the hood, and he glanced back at the house. Audra would know they were talking about her, about her case, but he didn't want her hearing it even if she knew the topic.

"Can you look in to her mother? I imagine you've got enough background to go off of."

Laurel nodded. "Yeah. What I don't know I can dig up. And we'll keep digging on the fake identity. Vicky got the name of the gravestone supplier, so she's chasing down the payment information there today. If it's the same name, we'll keep picking at it until we hit something."   .

"I'm getting reports from the fire department about last night. Hopefully there's some more evidence than we've come across. Audra isn't wrong about people too often, and I don't think she has rose-colored glasses where her mother's concerned."

"But it's too big of a coincidence not to look in to," Laurel said, finishing for him.

"Yeah."

"She probably shouldn't be staying here."

He knew it, and it frustrated him, because he also understood why she was being stubborn about it. "She won't go."

Laurel studied the house, then him. "So I suppose you won't either."

"It's the job."

Laurel laughed. "Uh-huh. The *job*." She shook her head. "I give it six months."

"You give what six months?"

She opened her car door. "You know, I was pregnant by my first wedding anniversary."

He gaped at her before he found his voice. "What the hell is that supposed to have to do with anything?"

She shrugged. Held up a finger. "Worked a case." She held up another finger as she took a step back toward the car. "Fell in love." With every step, she held up another finger and gave another ridiculous point. "Got married. Kids one, two, three, four." Then she slid into her driver's seat. "You'll beat me, I bet. On a spread like this? I'm guessing five or six."

"What in the ever-loving hell are you talking about?"

Laurel only laughed and closed the car door, waved as she backed out of the drive. Copeland watched her go, figuring that she was just… Well, obviously she was just messing with him. What did he care about her life? Her kids?

Five or six. She was messing with him. And regardless of *any* of that, he had things to do. Like stick to Audra so she was safe. Like stop whoever was trying to scare her, hurt her, even if it *was* her mother.

Five or six. Laurel was out of her mind. And just *messing* with him. He stomped back into the house. Audra was in the kitchen, where he'd left her with instructions to stay put, surprised that she'd done it.

But she was putting together some kind of breakfast. "I really need to go to the grocery store, but I found some waffles hidden in the back of the freezer," she said with fake, forced cheer. "I've got some chores that need handled first, but I suppose you'll want to come with me for both."

He wanted to tell her he didn't *want* to, but he was going to. But that would be a lie. He wanted to be where she was, and it was a problem that it wasn't only about safety.

"I don't like the idea of us leaving this place alone. It gives whoever is doing this time and access. Can't you have groceries delivered?"

She spared him a disapproving glance as she plated up the frozen waffles she must have toasted in the oven. "No one delivers groceries all the way out here, Copeland."

"We'll figure something out." If he had to he'd ask a favor of someone, since God knew she wouldn't. He'd figure it out.

She tried to take the plates to the table, but he grabbed them from her. She didn't look like she was limping quite so badly, but she could be putting on an act. He didn't know how it could possibly heal when she wasn't giving it rest.

He put the plates on the table, then looked back at her. She was just standing there, looking at the table. Misery and sadness were etched all over her face. She met his gaze with shiny blue eyes. She wasn't going to cry. He could tell from the way she held herself. But she wanted to.

"She's going to look in to my mother."

He could lie. Reassure. But it would be pointless and wouldn't help her any. "Yeah."

She put a palm to her chest, rubbed, like she was having pain. He couldn't stand that, so he crossed over to her, wrapped an arm around her like he had last night. Just comfort.

Maybe for the both of them, because her hurt did *something* to him. He wanted to fix it.

And that didn't mean there was *marriage* in anyone's future, or five or six *anything*. It was just…the moment.

She leaned against him. "I feel like someone took a whisk to my brain. It's all scrambled eggs up there."

"Great sex will do that to you."

She snorted out a laugh as he'd hoped. But then she sighed. "I know you're going to get mad at me, but I'm sorry. Sorry your coworker showed up here and saw…everything."

"Why are you sorry?"

"It must be embarrassing."

"Why would it be embarrassing?" He didn't think about Laurel and her sudden insistence on telling him about how she'd met her husband or how many kids they had. "There's nothing embarrassing about being with you, Audra." Maybe that was a little too naked, all in all, but she relaxed into him even more.

They stood there a few minutes in a pleasant kind of silence, the smell of waffles and syrup filling the kitchen. It was homey and nice and…just, *right*.

"Apparently I've got a soft spot for martyrs," he said, more to himself than to her, but she made a noise in response— half amusement, half despair.

"Well, that's something I guess." Then she moved up and brushed a kiss across his mouth. "Let's eat before the sad freezer waffles get soggy."

Yeah, it was a hell of a soft spot.

Chapter Fifteen

Copeland was true to his word in that he didn't let her leave his sight. Sometimes it was nice—an extra hand with the feeding and a repair she had to do on the north fence line, especially with her ankle still a little tender. Sometimes it was frustrating—when he told her she needed to stay off her ankle as if she wasn't the one dealing with the pain.

She didn't know how he did it, but he wrangled some-one from Fairmont to bring out a full load of groceries. She winced a little at the sheer number of bags he carried in. How was she going to afford all this food at one time?

But she forced herself to smile at him. "Impressive. How much do I owe you?"

"Nothing."

Her smile faded. "Groceries cost money, Copeland."

"They do, and since I'm here, eating your groceries, that you cook, by the way, I buy."

He said it in that way it was clear there was no arguing with him, which had anxiety creeping into her chest. She wasn't going to owe him, rely on him. She'd find a way to repay him. Maybe she didn't know the total, but she'd es-timate. And somehow, some way, she'd find a way to give him that money back.

"But before we get started on lunch or cooking, you've got something you have to do." He steered her into the living room, nudged her onto the couch, then set her laptop on the coffee table in front of her.

"What?" she asked, even though she knew. She knew and she didn't want to. Why did she have any affection for this man who was constantly pushing her to do the things she didn't want to?

"Call your sister, Audra. You don't think I know what time it is in Italy? You wait any longer, you'll be claiming you don't want to wake her up. Call her now. Tell her what's going on before she hears it from someone else."

Another order, in that same steely voice that was impossible to argue with. But she didn't need to argue to get her way. She'd learned how to get around the always-up-for-an-argument Rosalie. She did need to tell Rosalie *something*, but it didn't need to be everything. Just pertinent pieces, so if something *did* get to her, she didn't overreact.

Audra smiled placidly at Copeland. "I will call her—right now, in fact—if I can get some privacy."

"Nope."

Her smile withered into a scowl. "Copeland."

He stood there, handsome and obnoxious, arms crossed over his chest. "I'll stay out of the shot. You don't have to tell her I'm here, unless you want to. But you have to tell her everything else. And if you recall the deal—"

"Twenty-four seven. Yeah, yeah, yeah." How was she going to get around this now? She'd figure out something. She was quick on her feet, and surely Copeland understood the concept of leaving out a few details.

She pulled up the video-conferencing app and clicked Rosalie's name. Rosalie answered after only a few rings, her face popping up on the screen. She was framed by a pretty window with a bunch of buildings in the background. On the other side of the world.

It was so weird. Their whole lives since Rosalie had been born, they'd lived in the same house, been in each other's pockets, and then Rosalie had moved out last year and now she did things like jet off to Europe.

Audra knew some people probably thought she was jealous, but she wasn't. She didn't want to leave or go anywhere. But she was *so glad* Rosalie, with all her restless energy, was doing it. Especially with a husband who appreciated her just the way she was.

If there *was* jealousy, it was maybe there, in the doting partner, but Audra wasn't about to think about that with Copeland staring at her from across the room.

"Well, look at you, Ms. Italy," she greeted, forcing herself to smile.

Rosalie grinned. "It's probably sacrilege to say while I'm here, but I think you'd hate it."

Audra laughed in spite of herself. For all the different regrets she might have had about her life up to this point, staying put was never one of them. Even with danger swirling, this was the only place she wanted to be.

But Rosalie's smile faded. "What's wrong, Aud?" Rosalie asked, concern in her tone. "That's your fake smile. Stiff and weird. Which is concerning since Natalie and Norman had very similar smiles when we talked to them the other day. Everything's okay, right? With Vi and—"

"Vi's perfect and so is Fox. This isn't about them. Or Franny. Or anyone really. There's just some…issues with the ranch. I asked Natalie and Norman not to worry you about it. I'm handling it."

"You always do." But Rosalie was frowning. "What kind of problems?"

"You don't need to worry."

"I didn't ask if I needed to worry. And if you tell me what

kind of problems, I won't. Because I know you can handle it. If you won't tell me, that makes me think it's more than just the ranch."

"It's not. It's just…a few odd things. The power went out. We had some fence damage. A little fire in the shed."

Rosalie's forehead scrunched up. "That's a lot of odd things. How did a fire start in the shed?"

"Well, they're still trying to figure that out," Audra hedged.

"Who's they? Did they put the fire inspector on it? That means someone set it. Did someone set a fire in the shed? Who would do that? What's going on?" Rapid-fire demands. Exactly what Audra had wanted to avoid.

But she didn't scowl. She didn't let her frustration shine through. She smiled placidly and spoke calmly in return.

"Rosalie. It's fine. I'm sure they'll come back with some reasonable explanation." She was so deep in her lie she forgot Copeland was there. Until he said her name.

She glared at Copeland, but he looked wholly unrepentant.

"Who's that?" Rosalie demanded, bringing Audra's focus back to the screen.

"Uh." Audra looked to Copeland, feeling helpless and stupid. If Rosalie knew Copeland was staying here…

"Tell her or I do," he said with absolutely no softness or give.

"Alright. I'm getting freaked out, Audra. Who the hell is that *guy* and—"

"It's Copeland," Audra said flatly, trying to keep her sheer fury at him out of her tone. "The fire was set by someone. Hawk Steele is looking into it. All the other problems we've had here are *small* and *petty*, but someone is doing them, and Copeland is investigating."

Rosalie's expression was *all* worry now. "You've got a

detective and a fire inspector investigating these so-called odd things. That's not *odd*, Audra. It's threatening and dangerous. How long has this been going on?"

She was going to lie. It would have been so easy to lie, but Copeland was glaring at her and he was going to undercut the lie if she told it, which would make things worse. Damn him.

"Just…a few weeks."

"So the *whole* time we've been gone? Oh my God. We're coming home."

"Rosalie, no."

"I'm ready to come home. I miss everybody, and I want a whiff of Fox before he doesn't smell like newborn anymore. This is a better reason than me just being whiny and homesick. We're coming home."

Audra blinked back tears. What a failure this was. "I wish you wouldn't."

Rosalie fixed her with a stern expression through the computer. "I've had a three-week tour of Europe with my exceptionally hot husband. Who can certainly afford to change our plans. Feeling guilty I didn't get the last week is stupid and insulting. Where's Franny? I want to talk to her too."

"I… She's in Washington."

Rosalie's expression went to furious. "Damn it, Audra. Tell Franny about this. You shouldn't be alone when someone is… I don't know what this is. Petty pranks? Except it's causing damages. You cannot be alone. Go stay with Norman and Natalie."

"No."

"Audra."

"Rosalie, I'm not here alone. I have everything handled, like I always do. I have involved any authority who needs to be involved, and nothing bad has happened to me. I'm not in any *danger*. It's just…something. The right people are looking in to it, and I am fine."

"If you're not alone, who's staying with you?"

When Audra didn't answer right away, Rosalie's eyebrows went up and she leaned forward. "This is serious enough that you've got the police staked out at the ranch?"

She couldn't let Rosalie think that, not that she wanted Rosalie to think other things. She just… Oh, she hated Copeland for putting her in this situation. "That's not exactly it."

"What exactly could it…" Rosalie trailed off, her eyebrows still drawn together in a confused kind of expression. Then she leaned even closer to the screen, lowered her voice to a whisper.

"You and Copeland?"

Audra flicked a glance at him over the screen. He was in the same exact position. And she felt…a million conflicting things.

"No. Yes. Sort of." She shook her head, irritated she was so mixed-up. "I can't have this conversation with you while he's glaring at me from across the room."

"Copeland Beckett, if you hurt my sister, I'll gut you like a fish," Rosalie shouted, as if he couldn't hear everything that was going on anyway.

Copeland sighed, walked over and took a seat next to Audra so he was in the frame. "Don't worry, she's bound and determined to hurt herself before anyone else gets a chance."

Rosalie scowled. "Sounds about right. We're on our way home. You both better be in one piece when we get back."

"It's a promise," Copeland said, all cop seriousness. But the hand he put over hers on the couch wasn't *cop* at all.

Audra didn't know how she could be so bone-deep angry at him…and still want to lean into that touch and him and believe his promise held weight.

When she knew exactly what believing did.

COPELAND SAT ON the couch, waiting for Audra to yell at him once she'd carefully closed the laptop after saying goodbye to Rosalie.

But she only sighed. "Well, I hope you're happy," she muttered, pushing to her feet.

Copeland's gaze followed her, but he didn't get off the couch. He didn't know what part of the conversation she was referring to, but it didn't matter. "I am."

She didn't say anything. Didn't lay into him. She just got that very prim, cool look about her. "I suppose we should eat some lunch."

It reminded him of last year, when Rosalie had been in the hospital getting stitched up and he'd gone in to give her an apology. Audra had watched him like he was the gum she'd scraped off her shoe.

It didn't bother him if she looked down at him in this moment. He'd done what was right, and if she wanted to get all prissy about it, that was her choice.

But he saw the anger flashing in her eyes that she was trying to hide. So he leaned back on the couch, crossed his arms behind his head, adopted his best dispassionate tone.

"You can tell me how you feel about it. It won't change anything, but a good yell or tantrum might make you feel better."

She blinked once, a flicker of her anger deep in her eyes before she iced it away. "Tantrum," she echoed.

"You can call it a lecture if it'd make you feel better."

"Nothing is going to make me feel better, Copeland," she said, every word bitten off with that ice, but underneath it was all flickering flame. "My sister is canceling her honeymoon over a few silly pranks."

"No, your sister is ending her month-long honeymoon a *little* early, because you, or this ranch that you won't leave, is under a credible and dangerous threat. If you want to turn that into some grand sacrifice on her part, that doesn't make it what's really happening."

She shook her head. "You don't understand, and you don't care that you don't. It's just 'I'm Copeland Beckett and I know everything.'"

If he knew everything, she'd be out of this mess. If he knew everything, he wouldn't be jumbled up in her life. If he knew *everything*, things here would be a lot different. But he didn't say that.

She whirled away from him. "I'm so angry with you right now. Screw your twenty-four seven. You've crossed every line. Pushed every boundary."

Some of his detachment was starting to fade. He tried to fight back the anger because it wouldn't get through to her. It would just end up with them fighting, but damn, she pushed at all his buttons. So he stood, in an effort to channel his frustration into his body rather than lash out.

"Someone has to." Okay, maybe he was going to lash out, anyway. "Your lines and your boundaries suck." He wasn't handling this right. It didn't take a rocket scientist to know that, but he was pissed too. And she wasn't walking away from him while she was in danger, whether either of them liked it or not.

She whirled back around, hands curled into fists, eyes flashing with fury. "I beg your—"

"You built those boundaries to keep everyone out, so you couldn't be disappointed? So you could control everything? Spoiler alert. Both are part of life."

She fisted those hands on her hips. "Thank you for those wise words and a lesson I wouldn't have been able to fathom on my own. I've certainly never been disappointed or had all my control stripped from me."

"Get snarky all you want. You know I'm right. Rosalie knows I'm right. Franny and Vi and everyone else would side with *me*, if they knew, but they're too indebted to you to raise a stink about it. Me? I don't owe you a damn thing. You could have kept putting it off, but you know as well as I do, it wouldn't have gone away. You'd have to have told her all about it anyway, and you'd feel the same."

"Not if it was handled and over."

"Okay, how about this? Rosalie would have felt the same sense of betrayal, if not a little worse, if she came home to you having handled all this on your own without telling her. That what you're going for?"

"No. You're being a jerk."

"Kinda my MO."

Her shoulders slumped, her eyes closed, as if she was in pain. She shook her head. "No, it isn't. You only wish it was."

Ouch. Still, she could get her licks in and it didn't change anything.

She opened her eyes, fixed him with one of those lost gazes that just about scraped his insides raw.

"This is how I get through it, Copeland. All my life. This is how I function. You cannot just sweep in and try to change it. This is who I am."

She must not have realized how absolutely beat-down she sounded. She must not have realized that her *get through* was sad, and it was making *her* sad. "Maybe it's gotten you through, Audra, but that's about it. It *isn't* who you are. Take it from someone who has spent the past few years just *functioning*. It's not the same as living."

She turned to face him. "Is that what we're doing?"

"You think a what-are-we conversation is going to send me running?"

She wrinkled her nose, some of her anger and sadness fading into something else. "At least temporarily."

"Tough. Yeah, we're living. I'd say we're both discovering something we haven't had in a while, or maybe at all."

She blinked at him once, straightened in that way she had that reminded him of a bird ruffling its feathers. She opened her mouth, but no words came out, so she closed it.

There was something about all this—the ways she thought she could send him running, the ways she clearly didn't expect *anyone* to stick around, stick it out, had him going further than he probably needed to.

"I care about you, Audra. Do I know what to do about it? Hell no. Am I going to run away like some kind of coward because of it while you're in *danger*? Double hell no. I'm going to protect you, from whatever's happening and your own stubborn pride. Deal with it."

This time when she blinked, he saw the telltale sign of tears in her eyes. But they didn't stay there, some fell over onto her cheeks. Like little daggers to his heart.

"And stop crying, damn it." He crossed to her. Brought her into his arms. "I can't take it," he muttered into her hair. "It just kills me."

"I never cry in front of anyone, so it's all your fault." She sniffled as she leaned into him. He felt the tension in her shoulders ease a little.

He ran a hand down her spine. His heart just *ached* when it came to her. And he didn't particularly care to think of the state of his heart, how he was twisting it up in someone that was part of a case he was working. He knew he was just *asking* for trouble that would come once this whole thing was settled.

But he couldn't stop himself. Maybe he didn't want to.

When his phone rang in his pocket, he muttered a curse, eased Audra away so he could answer it. "Beckett."

"Hey," Laurel said. He could hear the sound of her driving, so she must have him on Bluetooth. "Vicky's going to send you the details, but I just got another bit of a something. Not a lead exactly, not Florida, but it's interesting. One of the names of Audra's half siblings just popped up. He's been listed as a missing person out of Idaho. I don't know how it'd connect exactly, but I want us to look in to it."

Chapter Sixteen

Audra felt like she'd been through some kind of very strange gauntlet. She knew about gauntlets that were all bad. Gauntlets that were mostly good—like when Vi and Thomas had gotten married, or Rosalie and Duncan had. Gauntlets that were terrible—when Dad had died, when Vi had been kidnapped.

But this was a mix of everything. Failure and depression over drawing Rosalie into this. Dread over having to tell Franny. Anxiety that they had no answers. And twin feelings of joy and terror that Copeland had stood across the room and said: *I care about you.*

How? Why? Was he lying just to keep her safe, just to do his job?

No. That wasn't him. As hard as it was to understand why he would care about her, she knew he wouldn't say it without meaning it. Not Copeland.

He was still talking into his phone. She got the impression it was to someone from work, probably Laurel. When he hit End, then slid the phone into his pocket, he took a minute before he turned and looked at her.

"Interesting development. Do you know anything about Austin Young?"

Audra tried not to frown. "I know Austin is the name of one of my half siblings." She thought back to what they'd learned after Dad had died, who she'd reached out to. "Not the youngest. The middle? I think he was in college when Dad died, but it wasn't a college I knew, so I don't remember the name. But he'd be out now, I'd think."

"He's been reported missing. He's been living in Idaho, but his sister, Karly, reported it from where she's living in Colorado. His mother and other siblings corroborated they hadn't heard from him, so the police did a welfare check. Boss hadn't seen him, friends hadn't seen him."

Audra tried to center herself with this new strange information. This Austin she shared half her DNA with but had never met had gone missing. "Karly. She's the oldest." Audra had reached out to Karly specifically, because they were almost exactly the same age.

There had been no response.

It didn't make sense that it might be connected. Idaho. Florida. "Do you think he...?"

"I'm not sure what to think yet, but there's something I want to cross off the possibility list." He studied her in a way that had her feeling wary. It was a *cop* study, like she was simply a piece of evidence to be slotted into place.

She didn't care for it, but a lot of it softened as he reached out, put those big hands on her shoulders. "Audra, I've got a big ask."

"Oh, an *ask*. How novel to not be *told*."

He didn't smirk or laugh or do anything else, which had dread curling in Audra's stomach. This was serious.

He held her gaze, and there was something warm and empathetic in his eyes, which made the dread dig deeper.

"I want you to call your mom."

Audra didn't allow herself to immediately react. She stayed very still, kept her expression frozen, until she could work through all the reactions inside of her.

"For the case," she said, very carefully.

"Yes. I want you to have a mostly normal conversation, but then I want you to ask if she knows someone."

"You think Austin missing connects…to my mother?"

"It could. She could. It more likely doesn't, but I don't want to leave that stone unturned. Something is coming out of Florida, where your mother is. Someone I was looking into went missing around the time all this started. I want to make sure those are two separate things."

Audra swallowed. "She wouldn't have anything to do with my father's other kids. She won't even…"

"Have anything to do with her own?" he asked, finishing gently for her.

She couldn't hold his gaze, and even she knew the little shrug she'd meant to be casual was nothing but jerky under his hands. "Yeah."

"Categorically her loss, Audra. But you know that."

Did she? She wanted to know it, but sometimes… Sometimes it all just felt like she'd been rejected over and over and over again by everyone.

Not Rosalie. Not Franny. Not Vi or Magnolia. Not… Copeland.

Not yet, anyway.

She shook away that thought. "I could call her. I will, if that's what you need for the case, but we don't usually talk. There'd be no reason for me to call her up, unless I tell her I think she's the one terrorizing the ranch and I don't think that's going to go over well."

Copeland shrugged. "Tell her you want her to come up. Meet your new boyfriend."

She wrinkled her nose. "*Boyfriend.* That makes us sound like teenagers." Not that he'd said *he* was the boyfriend. It was just a conceit.

"You got a better word?" he asked, like…

"No." *Boyfriend.* But Copeland wasn't that. He was…

He wasn't saying they were though. He was saying to tell her mother they were as an excuse.

"She wouldn't even come for Rosalie's wedding. Why would I think she'd come to meet a boyfriend?"

"Just pretend you live in eternal hope she'll change her mind."

Audra knew her mother never would, but…"What if she says yes?"

"What if she does? I can meet your crappy mom, Audra. I'd even be on my best behavior. Mostly."

Audra didn't have the slightest clue what to say to that. To making it feel like a real thing when it wasn't. It was all too muddled and confused. Pointless to think about. Mom wouldn't come. She didn't have any connection to Austin.

But Copeland's hands were still on her shoulders. He gave them a squeeze. "The word *boyfriend* doesn't bother me. I don't shake easy, Audra. Not once I'm dug in. And I'm getting pretty damn dug in."

She wanted to cry again, but it was getting ridiculous. The whole thing was ridiculous and… *Dug in.* She didn't know how. Couldn't understand *how.* But she supposed, as much as it terrified her, he deserved a little of the same certainty.

"Me too."

"Good." He squeezed her shoulders one last time. "Let's call your mom."

HE DIDN'T LIKE this version of her. The hurt version. The woman who'd been failed by too many people who should have loved her unconditionally. Watching a woman as caring and sweet as Audra dread calling her own mother twisted his guts into knots.

But this had to be done. He had her put the phone on speaker before she dialed her mother.

"She might not answer," Audra said as it began to ring. She kept her gaze on the phone sitting on the table, clearly hoping for that eventuality.

"Then leave her a message to call you back."

"She might not—"

The ringing stopped and a woman's voice scratched out from the phone receiver. "Audra."

"Mom. Hi."

"Is everything alright?"

"Yeah, of course. I just… It's been a while. I wanted to check up on you."

There was a beat of silence. Copeland could almost *hear* the suspicion in it. "Well, I suppose it's about time."

Audra linked her hands together. Her head was bowed, no doubt to hide the misery on her face, but he didn't need to see her expression to know this was a misery to her.

"Rosalie's wedding was beautiful. Did you get the pictures I sent?"

There was a kind of sniffing noise. "Easy to be beautiful when your husband is loaded," she said bitterly. "But you know, I'm seeing someone myself."

It was petty and superficial. Childish, really. Copeland couldn't believe the woman on the other line was a mother, let alone the mother of adult children. Once this case was over, he was going to send his mother flowers as a thank-you.

"I suppose Rosalie thinks she wins with a baseball player and his boatload of money, but my Isaac? He's a burgeoning artist. He's going to make such a splash."

"Oh, that's…great, Mom."

"It is," the woman said firmly, but Copeland's mind was whirling.

He'd been looking in to all of Audra's half siblings, so he knew bits and pieces about them. Like that Austin worked at an art gallery in Boise and was attempting to become an artist himself.

A coincidence. It *could* be, but what kind of insane coincidence was that?

"Is there anything else, Audra? I am very busy."

"Oh. No, I guess not. I just…heard recently that one of my half siblings has gone missing. Austin. He's the middle one I think and—"

"I can't believe you'd even utter that name to me."

"I'm sorry," Audra said, in what was clearly an automatic, knee-jerk apology. "It's just…upsetting and made me think of you. Worry about you."

"And you think I'd care about *that*? After all the *upsetting* your father put me through? With that *other family*? Honestly, Audra, what *are* you thinking?"

"I suppose I wasn't. I'm sorry." She pushed a finger into the corner of her eye, like a headache was drumming there, and Copeland had the acute stab of guilt that he was putting her through this.

But *art* and Florida suddenly had a connection, and they wouldn't have stumbled upon it without this little foray into the heart of Audra's pain.

"I have to go. This has been *very* upsetting. Next time you call, I don't want any topic that even remotely connects to your father. Do you understand me?"

"Yes, ma'am."

"After what he did. After… Oh, I'm so worked up now. That's what I get for taking a call from you. There is no reason to call me again unless it's *actually* important, Audra. And you can tell that to your sister too. Goodbye."

"'Bye, Mom." But it was clear the connection had ended before she'd even gotten the goodbye out.

Copeland fought the urge to bundle her up and just hold on until this all went away. But it wasn't going away, and they had to get to the bottom of this more than deal with her completely understandable issues.

He'd send his mother two bouquets of flowers.

"Well, no need to use the boyfriend excuse," Audra said. She sounded very much herself, but he could see the way she chose each word carefully. The way she held herself just so, as if she was still enough the pain couldn't get through. "She was too busy bragging about hers." Audra sighed deeply, closing her eyes and leaning her head on the back of the couch. "She doesn't know Austin, Copeland. You heard how she reacted. She's not connected. She can't be."

"Do you know what your half brother does for a living?"

"Huh?" She opened her eyes, looked at him in confusion. "No. I don't…"

"He works at an art gallery in Boise. And does some of his own painting on the side with a clear desire to make it to the big time."

"That's…"

"A pretty big coincidence."

Chapter Seventeen

Even though he had leads to follow, Copeland didn't insist she stay put, like Audra expected. After they ate lunch, he insisted on doing her chores with her. Well, after she'd ripped off the Band-Aid and called Franny too.

No doubt by tomorrow she'd have a full house again. Would Copeland stay? Did she want him to?

Questions she didn't want to ponder right now. They had stalls to muck, and she really wanted to tell him he didn't need to help. She *really* wanted to tell him she could handle this. She just had to find a way to explain it to him in a way that didn't sound like martyring herself.

"If something comes up that you need to handle—"

"Relax, Audra. Laurel will handle it," he told her as they shrugged their jackets on. She'd scrounged up some very old work boots of her dad's in the stables and he was using those when they were out on the ranch.

"She's got Austin's information, the name Isaac and your mother's whereabouts to go off of," he continued, stepping outside with her. "I'll look in to what I can later, once we're done with this, but if we're going through all the work of staying put, you might as well get your work done."

Audra didn't know what to say to that, because it made her feel guilty, but she also realized Copeland wasn't *trying* to. Which meant the guilt was her own doing, and she didn't love that realization.

They walked over to the stables in quiet. If she kept taking the ibuprofen at the correct intervals, her ankle mostly didn't bother her, which was a relief. Copeland barely even bugged her about it now.

Audra knew Copeland wore a gun, knew the way he walked, looked around, was all in that *cop* manner. Looking for threats. Looking for clues. But when they came to a stop at the stables, and she unlocked the padlock that kept the doors shut, she turned back to see him gazing out at the horizon. It wasn't the first time she'd seen him look out at it like that.

Not coplike. Not detached. Not seeking out a threat. But just…a soft kind of appreciation of the beauty all around them. Like he enjoyed it here. Could find some kind of belonging here.

Which was ridiculous, of course, and her fairy-tale heart complicating things just like it always did. Best to nip that in the bud.

She opened the doors, gestured him inside and went to gather the tools. She handed him his shovel, met his gaze with clear, determined eyes of her own.

"I'm sure Rosalie and Duncan will insist on staying here once they're back, even though they shouldn't. Add Franny and it's a full house. You won't have to stay here. I'll have help and constant babysitting."

He didn't say anything at first, just took the tool and turned to the first stall. After a few stretched-out moments, all he said was "We'll see."

Audra didn't know what the hell to do with that. So they worked in silence, cleaning up the stalls, brushing down the horses.

With her truck still out of commission—something she wished she'd taken care of or could get taken care of before Rosalie got back, but too late now—she'd need to take the horses to go back on a windbreak on the far corner of the property. It looked a little weak the last time she'd been up that way. She also needed to check on a few of the cows and make sure they weren't getting too thin with all this bitter cold. She'd need to do some separating soon if there wasn't a change there.

Lots to do, always, but the stall cleaning went quickly with Copeland's help. Once they were done, Audra surveyed his work. "You're not so bad at mucking stalls."

He grinned at her. "It's not such a bad chore. Kinda nice to do something physical outside of a gym. The horses might even be growing on me."

"Well, good, because we're going for a little ride to check on some things."

He agreed easily, helped her with saddling them up. He seemed interested to learn, not just help, which Audra didn't know what to do with. Rosalie helped with the ranch a lot, didn't require any teaching, but there was no love there. No *interest*. It was a duty and duty only for her.

Franny offered to help, but her head was in the clouds and it was usually easier for Audra to handle it herself and let Franny tackle any household tasks she felt necessary.

Sometimes Norman or a hand from the Kirk Ranch came over and helped, but Audra always made sure she returned the favor. She wouldn't let herself grow debts that made people resentful, like her parents had.

So she didn't know what to do with Copeland's interest, pleasant attitude, or aptitude for the chores and the riding. Except take things one step at a time.

They rode out to the windbreak, and as Audra suspected,

part of it had fallen over. She'd need to nail some boards back into place. She gave Copeland a few instructions, hauled her tools out of her saddlebag and then got to work.

It would have been nearly impossible to do on her own. She probably would have been forced to call Norman. Then she'd have felt she owed him a favor, and that would have sat like an uncomfortable debt there in her brain.

Almost like you're your own problem, Audra.

But what if she couldn't handle it all? Everything would fall apart. She'd been holding everything together for as long as she could remember. She was the glue, the foundation. Without her...

She rubbed at her chest. It was getting tight, and while she wasn't *prone* to them, sometimes when things were especially stressful, she suffered a panic attack or two. But she handled it. She always handled it. And no one knew, because she handled it.

But Copeland was right there, and she knew he sensed something was wrong when his arm came around her shoulders.

She breathed carefully, kept her expression as neutral as possible. When she trusted her voice, she gestured at the windbreak. "We do good work."

"Yeah. And this really helps the cows stay warm?"

She nodded, some of the tightness in her chest easing. "Yep. Next up, we've got to check on a few of them. If they get too thin, they'll have to be separated so I can ensure they're eating and can give them some winter supplements."

"And if this was some random winter, with no threats, you'd just be handling all of this on your own."

"I have help."

"When and if you take it. Big *whens*. Big *ifs*."

She wanted to get away from him, but his arm was holding her in place. She squinted at the mountains in the distance. She couldn't put into words the *need* to do all that. It came from a place too deep to fully verbalize.

And if she tried to tell him, it felt like it would uproot the strength of purpose that kept her going.

"I have no doubt a lot of people around you know this, that maybe even tell you this, and you probably don't listen to them, and you probably won't listen to me, but it's impressive what you do, what you handle. All on your own."

It was just the kind of compliment that should have touched her. Instead, it made her want to shrug away the words. Pushing every boundary, just like she'd accused him of earlier.

"Would it kill you to take a compliment, Audra?"

God, sometimes it felt like it might.

"I know they did a number on you, but it doesn't have to keep doing the same number."

"He says, from experience," she grumbled, only half-irritated. Because it was true. Both what he said, and where he'd come up with it. They weren't trite words. It was his own experience.

Someone had done a number on him, and he'd changed his whole life rather than live in the bowels of that.

"I'm getting there, I think." His arm stayed around her, that comforting warmth, this unknown glow of being able to let go, let someone else handle something when none of her usual get-arounds worked.

Because Rosalie was tenacious and demanding and sometimes managed to wheedle Audra into accepting some help, some credit, but mostly—because she'd grown up with Rosalie and knew all her tender points—she knew how to move around her sister.

She didn't know how to move around Copeland. Not when

he was poking into things that were about *her*, not the case. *Life*, not threats.

"You could get there with me, Audra," he said, very carefully. "All it takes is a little leaning."

She laughed, knew it was bitter-sounding. "Is that all? Because every time I've let myself lean, I've fallen flat on my face."

"You won't with me."

The worst part was she believed him, even when she knew she shouldn't.

THEY FINISHED HER CHORES, and while Copeland was eager to get back to the case, to find some answers for her, he'd also enjoyed himself in a weird way. There was something different about doing a lot of physical labor and seeing your efforts have physical manifestations. So much of his own work was nebulous. Sure, he solved mysteries, helped people out of danger, but then it was left up to the mess of the judicial system.

The only thing that could undo the windbreak was Mother Nature.

He glanced at Audra as they walked from the stables to the house. Speaking of things that needed an act of nature to move.

She needed a push, and it wasn't coming from the people she'd learned to fool with her walls and boundaries.

So it was going to have to be him.

Something he'd think about later, when there wasn't a strange car in Audra's drive.

He stopped her progress, situated himself in front of her. Rested his hand on his weapon. "You recognize that car?"

"No."

A woman got out of the driver's seat. Copeland gestured

for Audra to stay put, and he did the same, watching as the woman crossed the yard with purposeful strides.

"Hello. I'm looking for Detective Beckett."

"You found him."

The woman smiled, and there was something about the eyes, almost the same shade as Rosalie's, that had him more wary than the sudden appearance of a stranger. She held out a hand as she approached, offered a firm handshake. Cop or military, he was almost certain.

"My name is Karly Young. It was brought to my attention that you've been looking in to my brother."

Definitely the same blue eyes. He glanced back at Audra. She looked a little pale. But she stood there, strong as ever, ready to face something she shouldn't have to face.

"Bent County is a bit of a hoof from Schriever." He'd looked into all the half siblings, so he knew Karly *was* military, currently working at a Space Force base in Colorado. He wanted her to know that he'd looked in to her as well as her brother. Maybe this was innocent, but he wanted her to know he wasn't caught unaware.

"I suppose it is, but I'm desperate to find my brother. You were looking in to him before he was reported missing."

Copeland studied her. "Where'd you hear that?"

She smiled, maybe a little ruefully. "I know people. I want to know your connection."

Copeland gestured at the house behind him. "You really going to pretend like you don't know the connection?"

Karly's expression hardened. Copeland noted she had expressly not looked in Audra's direction.

But Audra clearly couldn't resist. "It's cold," she said from behind him. "You should both come inside and have this discussion."

The woman—*Karly*—looked at the house. She did not look at Audra. "No. Thank you." The words were clipped. Icy.

Hurt crossed over Audra's face, and it made him want to be difficult with Karly for the sake of it, but that wouldn't get them answers.

He weighed his questions, his next moves. Decided being forthright without explanation was the best course of action. "What connection does Austin have to Florida?"

Karly frowned. "None."

He could have played along, but he was tired of Audra living in a world of nonanswers, so he didn't even play that game. "That isn't true, and I know it. So you can either give me the truth, or you can leave."

He watched the woman's face. Hints of Audra, but something harder and sharper. Angrier. There was a deep-seated bitterness there that even when Audra found some bitterness within her, didn't twist like this.

Copeland found his hand creeping back up to his gun. There was something about this woman he didn't trust.

But some of that softened. Not into anything *soft*, but something far more resigned. Karly looked back at her rental car, shook her head.

"Some internet girlfriend. He'd talked about visiting her in Fort Myers. Honestly, the first day he was missing, I figured that's what he'd done. But I can't find any evidence he went to Florida." Everything in her expression went hard again. "I want to know where my brother is."

"So do I," Copeland returned. "Would your brother have any reason to want to harm this place?"

"Of course not." But Karly's gaze looked at the boarded-up house windows. The plastic-wrapped truck windows. "You've had trouble."

Copeland could have corrected her. Pointed out it was

Audra's trouble, not his. But it felt a little too tenuous. So he kept talking to Karly like Audra wasn't there, even though he knew it hurt all of them. "Lots of it. Coming from some-one who has connections to Florida." Something occurred to Copeland then. Maybe Karly didn't know what her brother was up to, but she had the background.

"When your dad was alive, did he give your brother any reason to think this ranch was his?"

She snapped right back up—all bristle and offense in-stead of any hint of exhaustion or defeat. "I don't have to answer these questions. I came looking for my brother, and I want to know why you were looking in to him before he disappeared."

"You're looking at it," he said, pointing at the boarded-up windows.

"Then you're a really bad detective," Karly snapped, then turned on a heel and headed back toward her car.

Chapter Eighteen

Audra didn't think. She just acted. Because she'd never been this physically close to anyone from her dad's other family. Every overture she'd made since he died had been met with refusals or silence.

But Karly was here now. *Here*. And Audra wasn't about to let that go. She followed her, pulling away from Copeland's attempt to stop her. She moved between Karly and the car so Karly couldn't get in and speed away without some kind of altercation.

"We're sisters," Audra said firmly.

But Karly appeared wholly unmoved by the word. "All you are to me is a reminder my dad wasn't who he was supposed to be. I don't need that in my life. Sorry."

She didn't sound sorry, and maybe that's what had Audra's temper straining. Or maybe she was emboldened by the fact that Copeland stood back, didn't try and interfere or step in now.

"He wasn't who he was supposed to be to us, either. You aren't special or unique. We're all in the same Tim Young shipwreck."

"Maybe. We want to use that metaphor? My brother is lost at sea, so I've got more pressing concerns than someone else's wreck." Karly looked her up and down, like Audra was the center and cause of everything their father had done. It sent a cold chill through Audra.

"I'm sorry," Audra said, and she meant it. As frustrating as this was, she understood more than anyone what it was like to be her—*their*—father's victim. "I'd like to help."

Karly shook her head. "I didn't come here for help."

"Then what *did* you come here for?"

Karly's eyes darted to the house behind them. The broken windows. Audra couldn't read the expression, but it wasn't *neutral*.

"You knew this existed," Audra said, striving to keep her voice even. "I invited you all here. I wanted… I wanted us to see if we could be a family."

Karly snorted bitterly. "Benevolent of you."

Audra shook her head. "No. I was trying to find some way to mitigate the grief of losing him twice. The finality of *death*, and the death of the man I thought he was. Which wasn't all that great. I wasn't under any illusion he was great. He was selfish. He was careless. He was so many crappy things, and caused me a lot of pain and strife, even before I knew he had a whole other family." The next words stuck in her throat. She didn't want to admit them, but she saw Karly's stonewall expression and knew the only way through was to find some common ground. "And I still loved him."

Maybe Audra was taking it too far, but in the grand scheme of things, couldn't Karly see that the man between them was the enemy? The man who'd put them both in this position and got to die rather than deal with any of the fallout.

Karly swallowed. Hard. The anger, the bitterness, the sharp edges didn't dull, but something in her…slumped.

"Okay, yeah. Maybe Dad talked about his ancestral home." Karly scowled at the house, encompassed it in one dismissive gesture. "Weaved big, tall tales about the Wyoming ranching life. How someday, it'd all be ours." Her hard blue gaze turned to Audra. "I didn't buy it then."

Audra inhaled sharply, because the implication was clear. "But Austin did."

There was a war playing out on Karly's face. A face that had little hints of Dad in it—the sharp chin, the blue of her eyes Audra often saw in her own reflection. Little things that reminded Audra of Rosalie—the way her mouth turned down in anger, the arch of an eyebrow.

Audra didn't know how the word *sisters* couldn't mean anything to her.

"If Austin did this," Karly said in almost a whisper, "I'm sorry. Dad's death hit him hard. He's…" She blew out a breath. "He's spoiled. Only boy."

Audra supposed she should have some sympathy since Dad's death—or the secrets that had uncovered—had hit them *all* hard, but…maybe that was why she couldn't work up any. "Only boy on both sides."

Karly's eyes fixed on hers, hard and cold. "I don't want there to be sides. I don't want you to exist."

"I guess that's too bad, because I do."

"Not to me." And with that, Karly sidestepped her and opened her car door. Audra didn't know what else to do but let her.

It wasn't a confession exactly, but it certainly added to the idea that Austin might be behind this. Ancestral homes. Ties to Florida…and yes, Mom lived in Fort Myers because of course she did. Spoiled men ruining the lives of the women around them.

Audra refused to let her life be ruined, even if it felt a bit like her heart was breaking all over again as Karly drove away.

Copeland came up behind her, put his hand over her shoulder and gave it a comforting squeeze. He didn't say anything.

Didn't offer any trite words. Didn't try to make it okay. He just stood there behind her, like some kind of...pillar.

She didn't let herself have any pillars that weren't her own two feet anymore. He was making that hard. He was making it seem like for once, for *once*, she really could depend on someone without losing her own sense of self.

Which was scarier than everything going on with Karly and Austin, so she focused on her half siblings rather than everything she was feeling for Copeland.

"I'm glad, in a way," she said to him, even as she still watched where Karly's car had disappeared. "To meet her finally. I never could understand their point of view when it was just a refusal to talk to us. I still don't fully grasp it. Ignoring something doesn't change it. But at least I see that's what they're doing. If they pretend Rosalie and I don't exist, they can pretend he wasn't what he was."

"They're not doing that great of a job of pretending though, are they?"

Audra shook her head. This visit hadn't made much sense, but she tried to put herself in Karly's shoes. What if Rosalie wanted to do something stupid? What if she wanted to hurt the other siblings in some way? Would Audra have been able to stop her?

No.

Would she have excused her?

Audra didn't *love* the fact she would have. She would have done anything to protect Rosalie from mistakes born of her own grief. Which told Audra everything she needed to know about Karly and this visit.

She turned to face Copeland, met his gaze with her certainty.

"She came all the way here, this place she doesn't want to exist, not for me. Not even *about* me. She came because she thought *you'd* be a lead to him since you'd tried to investigate him."

Copeland's response was measured. "Maybe."

"But I don't think she's worried about his safety, or the fact he's missing," Audra continued. "She's worried about what he's going to *do.*"

"Or what he's already done," Copeland said darkly. His expression was as hard as his words and Audra hugged herself against all the *cold* she felt.

"Why… It still doesn't make any sense. I reached out. I tried to… I would have invited them in. I would have…shared just about anything." Emotion hitched in her chest, but she'd be damned if she was going to cry again. "And why is my *mother* involved, however unwittingly?"

He reached out again, pulled her into him. He was always doing that. Offering a hand, a squeeze, a hug. She had never considered herself a particularly physical person—it wasn't how she or Rosalie were raised, and while they might hug on occasion, while they were *easy* together, it wasn't like this.

Because you never let yourself lean, Audra.

And she knew she shouldn't. There was a deep-seated knowledge this was wrong, but there was something new undermining it. She hadn't meant to let him in, hadn't meant to trust him, fall for him. She knew it was a bad, *bad* idea, but she couldn't seem to help it.

Because he held her close, smoothed a hand down her spine. And she knew she was safe here, even if she tried to convince herself she couldn't lean on anyone outside her tiny little circle.

"We're going to get to the bottom of it," he said firmly. He pulled her back, but only enough so he could look into her eyes. "Whether she's covering for him or something else, she made a tactical error. She came here. She gave us something to go on. And we're going to go on it."

He was so certain. So determined to press that certainty

upon her. So good at being there, no matter how she tried to convince him he didn't need to be.

She knew she shouldn't. She knew she would regret this. Leaning. Trusting.

Loving.

But it was already there. So she moved forward, onto her toes, pressed her mouth gently to his. "Thanks," she murmured, against his mouth.

He held her close, kissed her again before tucking her head under his chin. "Anytime."

THEY WENT IN and ate dinner. Copeland sent an email to Laurel, updating her on everything and requesting more background information on Karly Young.

It felt clear Austin was the threat, but there was something about the woman and her visit here that just didn't settle right. He needed to know about her, just as much as he needed to track down Austin Young.

It was a gut feeling, and Copeland always trusted his gut. Occasionally, it led him astray, but no investigation was so straightforward a detective didn't take some wrong turns along the way. It wasn't about doing everything *right*. It was about knowing how to recalibrate if you went a little wrong.

After dinner, Copeland decided Audra needed a little bit of a breather from *everything*. Maybe it was a selfish decision, but he'd never claimed to be anything else.

He talked her into the shower, together, and loved that he was able to make her laugh—and tremble—as the specter of everything haunting them was pushed away for a little while. They curled into her lumpy bed together—she really needed to take better care of herself—and slept.

Copeland woke with a start to the sound of someone in the house. In less than a second, he had his gun in his hand and was out of the bed. Audra had barely stirred when someone shouted from out in the hallway.

"Audra!" It was Rosalie's voice, immediately followed by the bedroom door slamming open. Copeland breathed through the moment of panic and the thought that if Rosalie hadn't *yelled* before she'd opened the door, he might have shot her.

Rosalie made a distressed sort of noise, threw her hand over her eyes. "Oh my *God*. Gross."

Fighting his own embarrassment, the mix of relief and terror coursing through him at being awakened so suddenly, Copeland surreptitiously slid the gun back onto the nightstand shelf, where Rosalie wouldn't be able to see it and worry even more.

Maybe Audra *had* rubbed off on him.

He picked up his pants and pulled them up. Audra was scurrying out of bed now while he collected his shirt and pulled it on.

"Rosalie… How… You weren't supposed to be here until this afternoon."

"Yeah, well Duncan greased some wheels. We picked Franny up on our way too." She dropped her arm with some trepidation, and aimed a wrinkled-nose expression in Copeland's direction.

But Audra had already gone into full big-sister mode. Had he thought she wouldn't? She was moving toward Rosalie, arm outstretched. "Let's go downstairs. I'll put something together for breakfast. You and Duncan must be exhausted. You should head on home and rest."

Rosalie didn't budge. She stared at him over Audra's shoulder, like she could "gut him like a fish" with her mind.

He didn't wither. Did *she* think *he* would?

"Rosalie."

Rosalie finally looked from Copeland to Audra. "We're going to all go downstairs and talk this through," Rosalie said firmly. "And regardless of the outcome, just know Duncan and I are staying here until things are settled."

"Rosalie."

"Try to stop me," she replied firmly. Then hooked her arm with Audra's and sailed out of the room, dragging her sister along behind her.

Audra looked back at him a little helplessly, but he only shrugged. He didn't mind more bodies here. More help. Anything and everything that upped the odds of keeping Audra safe worked for him. Even if it was bound to be…awkward.

He could handle awkward.

Copeland followed them down at a safe distance. When he reached the bottom of the stairs, Franny had already engulfed Rosalie and Audra in a hug so that the three women held on to each other and swayed gently. They spoke in low, private tones. He didn't have to hear the words to know Rosalie was chastising Audra, and Audra was assuring Rosalie and Franny that everything was fine.

Copeland found himself…relieved. Maybe she was only giving them half truths, but here were two women who cared about her, who would *try* to take care of her. She wasn't as solitary and alone as she'd seemed this past week.

Had it only been a week? How had she upended everything inside of him in a few days? It didn't make any sense. He hadn't been looking to be upended.

But here he was.

He glanced at the man who came to stand next to him. Duncan Kirk surveyed him. Copeland had once watched this man play baseball on national TV. He'd always been a fan, though he'd never let Duncan know it. Especially when he'd been investigating the murder over at his parents' place last year.

So Copeland figured he deserved the clear lack of friend-liness on Duncan's face.

"Beckett," he greeted, but coolly.

Copeland matched his tone. "Kirk."

"We've got everything under control," Audra said above Rosalie and Franny's demands. "The police are looking in to a few leads, and nothing violent or dangerous has really happened. It's all small, petty things."

Rosalie turned to face Copeland with a glare. "Is she tell-ing the truth?"

Audra looked up at him helplessly, and no doubt his loy-alty was to Audra, but he also knew what she wanted from him wasn't right.

"There's a lot of truth to what she's saying," he agreed. But he couldn't help the *full* truth. "She's also downplaying it."

Audra stiffened, aimed a glare at him. But he could only shrug. "You are. There haven't been any physical threats made to her, that's true, but they *are* threats all the same. And you never know when threats will go too far."

Rosalie looked angry. Franny looked distressed. And Audra got that detached queen-of-the-manor look about her.

"There's no need to worry—"

"There *is* need to worry," Copeland interrupted her, even though it earned him an icy glare. "But there's no need to panic. We've got leads. We've got strings to pull. Which is an improvement. That doesn't mean we can be careless…" He moved his gaze from Rosalie and Franny to Audra. "Or martyrs," he added firmly.

That chin came up, shoulders back. She was pissed, but there was no way to get through this without making her angry. He already bent as far as he could by not making her leave. Everyone here needed to know how serious the threat was.

"I'm going to make some breakfast," Audra said, turning

on a heel and marching into the kitchen, Rosalie and Franny trailing after her with another round of questions.

Copeland made a·move to follow, but Duncan stepped in his way.

"You know, it seems to me, Audra is surrounded by family now," Duncan said, his tone polite, but very, *very* firm. "I'm not sure she needs you hanging around here unless it's official police business."

Copeland thought about that. How it would be easiest, maybe even best, if he took a few steps back. He could put everything he had, everything he was, into getting to the bottom of Austin and Karly Young. He could give her the space she likely needed, deserved.

But he'd never be able to focus if she wasn't in his sight. He'd be worried, every second of every day, that something had happened. Someone had gotten through. Something had snapped.

And more, he understood that she knew how to manipulate all these players. Maybe it wasn't a fair word, but she'd *maneuver* Rosalie and Franny, convince them everything was alright when it wasn't. She couldn't do that to him. Maybe someday she'd be able to, but not yet.

So he shook his head, even though he appreciated that there was *someone* in this world who was protective of Audra. Besides him.

"She might not need me," Copeland agreed easily. He didn't look away or let any of his own personal discomfort over his feelings show. Because maybe he was making every kind of mistake, the kinds of mistakes he'd made before, but for Audra it just wasn't possible to step away. "But she's got me."

Chapter Nineteen

Audra's temper fizzled through breakfast. Because Copeland was very clearly not welcome, but he settled himself at the table and filled in everyone on what had happened in a very matter-of-fact police way that didn't leave much room for Rosalie or Franny to overreact too, *too* much.

And she knew that was by design, not accident. He was trying to *help*, even when he was doing what she expressly wished he wouldn't.

She didn't know how to fight him. He was too…reasonable. Too fair. And she didn't know how to stay angry with him when he did things like sit at the breakfast table with just about everyone she loved and weather their hostility like it didn't matter to him in the slightest.

Which was something he probably dealt with at work plenty. Not everyone liked the law poking around, and not everyone liked what a detective might find. She could sit here and try to convince herself that was all it was—work.

But it wasn't.

"Whether she wanted to or not, Karly made it pretty clear Austin is our culprit. Or could be. We're working on tracking him down, seeing if we can prove it," Copeland explained in patient cop tones. "There's a lot of anger and bitterness there, so it tracks."

"Wow, they're so unique," Rosalie muttered, stabbing at

her eggs. "Bitterness. Anger. Over our SOB of a dad. Weird how I didn't think to take it out on the random kids we didn't know he had."

Those words settled into Audra differently, because hadn't she essentially said the same to Karly? They were the same. They were all victims of their father.

But the anger and bitterness she'd felt from Karly was geared toward *her*, toward the ranch. Not the situation. Not Tim Young.

With Rosalie back home, something about the entire interaction with Karly suddenly had a far more discordant note. Pretending someone didn't exist didn't mesh with anger. Anger was born of time and offense and hurt.

Then again, there'd been time—all these years—to nurture that hurt, so maybe it made sense, even if Audra didn't feel the same. Not everyone was going to react to betrayal in the same way.

But something was chewing at her, deep in the pit of her stomach. She'd make sense of it, but she needed…work. Cold air, animals, physical labor. Some alone time.

"I'd better get started on chores," Audra said, pushing back from the table. She wanted to clear the table, clean up after breakfast, but chores were more pressing and—

Duncan and Copeland stood, like they were some kind of partnered unit. Without even discussing it, they blocked her path.

"Duncan and I can handle it," Copeland said, like he spoke for *her* newly minted brother-in-law. And he must, because Duncan stood next to Copeland looking like just the same kind of brick wall.

"But—"

"Catch up with your family," Copeland said. *Ordered.* "And lock the door behind us."

She would have argued. She would have told him where to shove it, but he simply stepped forward, pressed a hard kiss to her mouth, then walked away, like that was that and he just got to…tell her what to do.

And kiss her in front of everyone.

She stood there, frozen with irritation and embarrassment and…something a lot warmer and nicer than those two things. But the darker emotions felt easier. Safer.

So why were the warmer, nicer ones winning?

"See?" Franny said, gesturing at Rosalie once the men were out of earshot.

Rosalie only scowled as she moved forward and locked the door.

"See what?" Audra demanded.

"You need someone bossy," Franny said with complete sincerity. "And hot. Copeland fits the bill."

"Bossy is obnoxious," Rosalie muttered before Audra could think of something to say.

They were moving around her. Everyone was taking over, and Audra simply didn't know what to do. It was like she was stuck in some vortex, some alternate reality, where she wasn't the one holding everything together.

"You say that because you're the bossy one in your relationship," Franny retorted as she began to clear the table.

Rosalie scoffed.

"Duncan's a marshmallow for you," Audra addeed with just a hint of wistfulness, unable to stop herself. Then she grabbed the rest of the dirty dishes and walked over to the sink. She wasn't going to be…helpless, frozen, *vortexed*. This was her life, her family, her ranch. She'd always been in charge of all those things.

Always.

"Oh, Duncan's plenty bossy." Rosalie wiggled her eyebrows until Franny and Audra were laughing, and it felt good. For her sister and cousin to be home. To be laughing.

But… She wasn't in control, and she didn't know what to do with that feeling. Except wrestling some of it back. She bumped Franny away from the sink. "You must be exhausted, rushing home. Why don't you go unpack and rest?"

"It was hardly a rush or a sacrifice. I can go back and visit my parents anytime, Audra." Franny bumped her right back out of the way. And then Rosalie slid in between them, like she was going to fight Audra off.

So Audra started in on her campaign to get Rosalie out of here. "I hope you know you don't have to stay here, and Duncan certainly doesn't need to help with my chores. Your house is just a stone's throw away. Franny's home and—"

"And you've got a detective cozied up in your bed?" Rosalie interrupted, arms crossed over her chest, expression somewhere between disapproving and assessing.

Audra wasn't sure what was going to happen now that everyone was back. She'd try to get Copeland to leave too. She'd have to convince him that she was well taken care of now, and he didn't need to be here twenty-four seven.

She didn't want to.

Which made saying the rest hard, but she'd swallow her pride if it got her sister living her very nice life over worrying about Audra's. "If it'll get you to go home and stop putting yourself out for me, he can stay here."

Rosalie rolled her eyes. "*He can stay here*, my butt. You couldn't get him out of here at gunpoint. Or you would have by now."

Audra opened her mouth to argue with Rosalie, but she couldn't find the words. Because she was a little too scared that she was letting her personal feelings for Copeland undermine all the strength she'd built up these past few years, which had been scary enough on its own, but with her family back it felt…dangerous.

Everything was flying out of control, and Audra needed to find a way to center it all, anchor it all, before…

Before *something*.

Maybe if she convinced everyone to leave her alone, she could accomplish something and feel more in control.

"I'm so glad you're both back," Audra said, forcing some cheer into her voice. "I wish you hadn't closed out your trips early, but it's good to have you home. And since you are, I just… I haven't had a moment to myself in days. I… I just need some alone time. To think things through. Copeland's been all up on this twenty-four-seven nonsense, and I haven't had a moment to myself."

She smiled hopefully at Franny, who kept her head bent and focused on washing the dishes. So she turned to Rosalie, who was scowling.

"How about this, just this once, for the slightest change, you try to *talk it through*, instead of isolating yourself and thinking through a problem without any help. I'm a private investigator, Audra. This is my *job*. I'm your sister. This is my family."

Maybe it was Karly firmly rejecting those terms—*sister, family*—that had Audra relenting. Because she liked to think she could maneuver Rosalie when she wanted to, but not when Rosalie sounded hurt. Not when there was someone who wanted to be her sister.

She let out a long breath. Maybe it was only fair to give Rosalie this, even if Audra wanted to handle it herself. Even if she wanted…

What the hell do you want, Audra? She felt like Copeland Beckett had swept into her life—on her own invitation—and jumbled it all up.

But Rosalie tugged on her arm, nudged her into a seat at the table. "I want to hear the whole story. The real story. From *your* point of view." Rosalie went to a drawer, pulled out a little notebook and a pen. "This might be Copeland's case, but it's mine now too."

"And once we're done with that," Franny said, settling herself on Audra's other side, "you can share the details on just what twenty-four seven with Copeland Beckett entails."

"It entails Copeland Beckett in his underwear in her bed this morning," Rosalie grumbled, clearly disgusted.

"Ooh," Franny said, clearly *not* disgusted.

The juxtaposition almost made Audra smile.

"First things first. Start at the beginning. No leaving things out to keep me from worrying. I'm worried. There's no more or less."

Audra really didn't want to, but it was clear Copeland wasn't going to let her minimize this to Rosalie, and Rosalie would get the details out of *someone*, one way or another. So Audra had no choice but to relent.

Which left her feeling...exhausted and like a failure. Something she was so tired of. So...over.

What if you stopped blaming yourself for everything?

She wanted to laugh, because the voice in her head sounded far too much like Copeland blaming her for being a martyr. Because she was. Because... Because by handling everything these past four years, she'd built her life on the crumbling foundation of her father's lies, and it wasn't earning her any awards.

What if she could...use this as a new starting point? What if she could...think about change, about *leaning* instead of all the holding tight that hadn't really served her?

It was *terrifying*, but she started with the very small step of telling Rosalie and Franny everything from the beginning, without glossing over things. Without downplaying or insisting it was fine.

Franny was gripping her arm by the time she got to the fire, and Rosalie looked like she was going to start throwing punches, but Audra forced herself to keep going. All the way to Karly's arrival and her interaction with their half sister.

Audra thought about the conversation as she relayed it. Those earlier thoughts about how odd it had been came circling back. "Karly said that Dad always talked about his *ancestral home*."

Rosalie snorted in disgust. "Yeah, fat lot he cared about that."

"He did though. Maybe not the way we wanted him to, but he did. And he signed it over to me a while before he died. Before his son would have been old enough to have any part of it."

"Not to protect you, Audra."

"No, I don't have any illusions about that. Because he told his son about it. His son who, according to Karly, bought in to the whole thing. So why did Dad tell his son about something he'd given me? Acted like he'd get it one day."

"Because he was a dick?"

Audra sighed. "Yes, but it's *more*, isn't it? If you set aside the hurt daughter and think like a PI. Copeland's trying to track Austin down, but he's missing, so we can't go to the source. If Karly knows why he told them, she won't say. So I have to try and think about this from Dad's point of view. If you're living two lives, how do you make sure they never connect?"

Rosalie shrugged. "Be a lying bastard?" She wrinkled her nose when Audra frowned at her. "Okay, okay. Think like a PI. You'd just have to make sure those lives never connect, right? They were in Idaho. We were here, and pretty isolated here at that. We had no reason to suspect anything, so…isn't it that easy when you're a lying bastard?"

"Maybe, but I'm starting to wonder… She was so angry. Karly. So bitter. About me, about us. She only came here because she thought Copeland would be a lead to Austin. And if Austin is the one doing this, that's even more than anger and bitterness. It's like…"

"Revenge," Franny said thoughtfully. "Blame and revenge."

"Yes. I guess," Audra said, nodding at Franny before turning her attention back to Rosalie. "Which means they both have so much anger and bitterness. No curiosity about us, about creating a relationship. And I know you weren't as gung-ho about reaching out as I was, but you weren't…angry at *them*, you know? Even at breakfast, you weren't…mad at *them*. You were mad at Dad."

"And still am."

"Sure, but don't you see what I'm saying? They've nursed these bad feelings. It's not ambivalence. It's…ire. And maybe they used that for these years since Dad died. Maybe they leaned on anger over grief and that's all there is to it."

"What other *maybes* are there?" Rosalie asked, but not like she didn't know, like she wanted Audra to say it. While her expression sharpened into that private-investigator look.

Audra shook her head. This was the thought she didn't like, but it kept poking at her. The *hate* in Karly's gaze. The rejection right after the funeral and every moment since. Where did that kind of rejection and vitriol come from? *Maybe* just grief. But maybe…

Audra really thought it had to be deeper than a secret brought to life. "Rosalie, what if they *knew*?"

"Knew…about us?"

"Yes. Before Dad died."

"You think Dad told them about us in an effort to keep us…divided? Apart?"

"I think it might make more sense than them being as blindsided as we were and as…closed off as they've always been."

Rosalie's expression softened into a hurt frown, not that her sister would ever admit it was hurt.

"That's worse," Rosalie said flatly. "I never thought a secret could be worse, but telling one side is *worse*."

"It is, and I'm sorry—"

"Don't apologize for him, Audra. You've done that enough."

She had. She really had. She didn't like to admit that taking on all the blame made her feel…safer. Safer than trusting and believing in anyone again. Safe to know you handled *everything*.

Safe, maybe, but not happy, not fulfilled. Hadn't Copeland said that? Surviving not living. Not…actually all that strong. Just safe in the most basic of ways.

But she hadn't felt *safe* since Copeland had swept in, broken down all her usual walls and boundaries.

Because, like he'd said yesterday, her boundaries sucked.

Audra let out a careful breath. "I'm going to change the subject for a minute. Because you guys are here, and Copeland isn't, and… I just…" She looked from her sister to her cousin, her best friends in the world. Rosalie's words about *talking it out* instead of figuring it out on her own rattling around in her brain. "I think I'm in love with him. I don't know how it happened."

Franny made a squealing sound and grabbed her hand, but Rosalie just regarded her with a detached cool gaze.

Audra swallowed at the lump in her throat. Tried to settle the terrified trip of her heart. "I've been trying really hard not to be," she whispered. "But he just…won't shake."

Rosalie inhaled, exhaled, slowly. Her gaze went to the door that Copeland and Duncan had exited out of this morning.

"Yeah, I guess I know the feeling," Rosalie muttered.

Audra's heart fluttered. Rosalie had been a little reticent about starting something with Duncan, and Audra had certainly given her a push in that direction, but that was different. That was…them.

"I don't think…all that is in our future, but—"

Rosalie turned on her in a quick sharp turn. "Why wouldn't it be in your future, Audra?"

Audra blinked, surprised at Rosalie's tone. "I don't know. Copeland and I are just…too different, probably." Admitting she'd fallen for him was one thing, thinking that meant a future was something entirely different.

"Yeah, and Duncan and I are two peas in a pod." She rolled her eyes. "Look, maybe I have my reservations about Copeland, but…if you care about him, and he cares about you, and he won't be shaken by the expert shaker, why are you already ruling out a future?"

"Aren't you the one who always told me I should stop believing in fairy tales?"

"And then I lived one, more or less. You were right, Audra, and you should be right for more than just me."

Audra wanted to believe that, but the bone-deep fear she couldn't was still lurking there. Still, arguing about it wouldn't get them anywhere. "Maybe," she said, managing to scratch out the word. "But, first… First, we have to figure this threat out. Whatever it is."

"It all centers around your father," Franny said gently. "And who knew him better than you, Audra?"

Which…actually gave Audra an idea.

COPELAND FOUND DUNCAN to be an easy enough chore partner. They didn't have to talk to get the work done, and it kept Audra safe and inside. He had a feeling Duncan had things he wanted to say, but he took his sweet time about saying them.

So Copeland maintained the easy silence, focusing on the work, and trying not to laugh at how…coming out and dealing with horses and cows and fences and the bitter cold had become *normal*.

And very nearly enjoyable.

They worked until it got close to lunchtime, but before Copeland could suggest going in for food, or checking in on Audra because the fact she hadn't come poking her nose into the chores despite his orders was downright *strange*, and had to be chalked up to Rosalie and Franny maybe tying her to a chair, Duncan spoke.

"It's too big of a place to keep secure. I know that from experience."

There'd been trouble at his parents' ranch next door last year, and since Copeland had worked part of the case, he knew Duncan had tried to install a lot of security measures, but still, things had slipped through the cracks.

"I agree," Copeland said, surveying the vast stretches of land around them. "There was a time I tried to convince her to leave, stay in town with Hart, or *something*, but now… I think staying is the right choice. As long as she's never alone. She's right that the threat isn't to her. I really do believe that. Someone wanted to scare her off. They didn't know her, and thought she'd scare easily."

"Not those Young girls," Duncan said with the ghost of a smile. Because even though Duncan had spent over a decade off in California being a professional baseball player, he'd grown up right here. Next door to the Youngs.

Which gave Copeland an idea. "What do you know about Tim Young?"

Duncan gave him a once-over, then shrugged. "Not much. Rosalie's version of him is a mustache-twirling villain, and he was a worthless SOB, don't get me wrong, but I don't have any insight into him that isn't that."

Copeland could press Audra on the details, but he kept... pulling back there. Maybe he needed to—

"My parents might," Duncan said.

"Would they talk to me?"

"If I told them to." Duncan squinted off into the distance, toward his parents' place to the east. "But they might be more forthcoming with me." He glanced at Copeland. "If you tell me what you want to know, I could go over there right now, probably get some answers."

Copeland considered. He'd rather do the questioning himself, but... Well, it made sense. Duncan was an insider. His parents would trust him to use the information wisely without second-guessing if they should be handing it out. Copeland was still an outsider, so they'd be more...careful.

"I want to know their impressions of him. Anything *they* know about the second family. I think it's pretty clear what kind of man he was, but I want to know...an outsider's point of view. What, if anything, they might have known or suspected about his second family."

Duncan nodded. "I can get that, if you think it'll help."

"Can't hurt." No, it couldn't hurt. "Maybe ask if there's anyone in town he was friendly with. Someone who might know more about that second family that I could question."

Duncan nodded. "Sure. I can go right now."

"Yeah. I'll finish up out here. And listen…"

"If you're going to tell me not to tell my wife about this, it's a no-go. And if you think she won't tell Audra...well, I think you know Rosalie better than that."

"He's a sore spot for Audra. She's got enough of those."

Duncan studied him with that same scrutiny he had since he'd arrived on the scene. "Some advice you didn't ask for.

You can't protect them from their sore spots, but you can be there when they hurt."

Copeland didn't have the first clue what to say to that. He supposed it was fair advice all in all. But right now, he had more important things to worry about than if Audra'd…let him be around for any hurts.

"I'll finish up here. You let me know what your parents say."

Duncan nodded. He put away his tools, gave Copeland a little salute, then headed off toward the Kirk Ranch on foot.

Copeland watched him go for a few minutes, trying to figure out his next steps. Rosalie and Franny were with Audra, and he had no doubt Rosalie wasn't letting her out of her sight. It gave him the chance to do a full perimeter check. Someone had to be coming in from somewhere to shoot the house, dig the holes, set fires, et cetera.

It wasn't coming from the front road. And he'd wanted to poke around the back of the property, but without her. Now was his chance.

Audra wouldn't appreciate him doing it alone, but he had his gun, and he was a *detective*. This was his job. He eyed the horse he'd been riding during his time here.

"Well, Bo, let's see what we can do on our own." He got the horse saddled and out of the stables, then mounted easily enough. "See? I'm a pro," he muttered to himself before urging the horse into a trot.

He rode out to the west fence, then trotted along the property line. He scanned the area around him for entrance and exit points. He studied the ground for misplaced footprints or tire tracks. He rode through a warming afternoon and felt the strangest sense of peace being on the back of a horse, in this gorgeous landscape. Almost like he belonged.

Something to think about, and maybe worry over, later.

He was coming up on the far back area of the ranch where he'd never been before. The land kind of changed, became overgrown with lots of stumps forming some kind of line. Was it a property boundary? He'd expected a fence, but—

The sudden explosion of a gunshot had the horse rearing, and since Copeland was reaching for his own gun in response to the shot, he didn't have a tight enough grip on the reins. He tumbled onto the ground with a hard, painful crash while the horse whinnied and galloped away.

Copeland swore, but he didn't have time to be hurt when he knew that had been a gunshot. Maybe it hadn't hit him, but it had been meant to he was pretty sure. He struggled to roll over to get his arm free to reach his gun. Pain shot down the arm, stars danced in his vision. Broken, no doubt.

He swore some more, then clamped his teeth together and got the gun in his left hand. He wouldn't be able to aim worth a darn with his left hand, but maybe it would be enough of a scare tactic to…

"Drop it."

The female voice was sharp. He heard footsteps approach, looked behind him at the overgrowth where a figure was emerging. Maybe he should have been surprised, but it just made too much sense.

"I wasn't going to hurt anyone." Karly Young looked down at him with those cold, flat eyes he'd *known* were trouble. "You shouldn't have looked in to me." She cocked the gun. "Now you've only got yourself to blame."

Chapter Twenty

Audra's head ached from the effort not to cry. They'd all gone up to her room, dragged out the tub of Dad's things, and the box of files Audra had kept for the ranch—just in case—then sat down on the floor to go through it together with an eye toward…

Well, she wasn't quite sure. Franny was right, though, it centered around Dad. So they had to dig in to what they had from the man and see if it sparked *some* idea of what was going on with his other family.

But it was mostly like digging in to an old wound she thought she'd healed, but instead had just festered under the scar of it all. Maybe she *was* bitter, she thought to herself as she shuffled through the paperwork of Dad signing the ranch over to her.

"He should have shared it," she grumbled.

"Why? We grew up here," Rosalie said. She was flipping through papers in another file. Taxes, maybe. When they were done, they handed things off to Franny, who organized them back where they belonged.

"You did *everything*," Rosalie continued. "Kept this place going when no one else would or could. Why should he have shared it with them?"

"Because they were his kids too. Like it or not."

Rosalie stopped her flipping, glanced at Audra. "Yeah,

I don't like it. But I guess you're right. Maybe they think we're the ones who kept it from them? Maybe that's why Austin is doing this."

"But then why not take my offer after the funeral?" Audra looked back down at the documents in her hand. Especially then, she would have... If they had even been remotely receptive to a relationship, no doubt she would have martyred herself then and there and given them all pieces of the ranch.

For good or for ill.

Would she now? She didn't know. Certainly not if Austin Young was the one behind these threats, and if Karly Young was the one trying to protect him... At the same time, she couldn't change the fact her father had other kids, that the Young Ranch was part of their family legacy.

And yet, how could she give up pieces of everything she'd shed blood, sweat, and tears over? Everything she loved?

It didn't matter because she didn't have the opportunity, and that above all else settled in Audra like a grudge. But maybe that was the core of all this—grudges, even if she didn't understand them.

"Wait. Did we know this?" Rosalie asked, scooting over to sit next to Audra. She held out a piece of paper. "He sold this back strip of land to the lumber company just a few months before he died." Rosalie held out the map, the bill of sale.

Audra studied the papers. "Oh, right. I do remember that. I was mad because he didn't run it by me first, but he said he needed the money. They cleared the land years ago, and it's mostly been empty ever since. Can't remember the last time I saw or heard anyone back there cutting trees or otherwise."

Which had a cold chill slithering through her. She thought back to the strange goings-on over the past few weeks, and wondered...

"When the windows were shot out, I didn't hear anyone

drive up or leave. Usually I can hear cars come and go on the drive. The gravel. The engines. The house just isn't that soundproof. I didn't hear anything. I chalked it up to being half-asleep, but what if they didn't come up from that way?"

It would make sense. The hole, the fire. Things that seemed impossible to do sneaking in from the road, or the boundary with the Kirks. But if the lumber company wasn't doing anything on the land in the back, couldn't someone set up a little home base there?

Rosalie was already on her feet and at the bedroom door before Audra could fully formulate a plan. But she knew her sister, and so did Franny, because they both jumped up at the same time and trailed Rosalie down the stairs.

"You can't just go running out there," Audra said authoritatively.

"Why not?" Rosalie replied. She went straight for the coat closet, where one of the gun safes was.

Audra's heart beat erratically, but she forced herself to breathe. To think. She knew the answer, even though it was… asking someone else for help. "We have to tell Copeland. He should have uniformed officers do it."

Both Franny and Rosalie slowly turned to face her, expressions registering shock. Audra tilted up her chin. "What?"

Franny wrapped her arms around Audra. "It *is* love," she said dreamily, earning her a bit of a shove from Audra.

"He's the detective on the case. This could be dangerous. It makes sense."

"Yeah, but when have you ever worried about being sensible? Come on, let's go see where—"

But Rosalie was cut off by the sound of the back door opening, so they filed into the kitchen.

It was only Duncan who entered. Alone. *Hours* after he

and Copeland had left. Audra felt one quick lurch of panic before she set it aside. She managed a smile.

"Where's Copeland? We've got something we want him to look in to."

Duncan stilled in the middle of moving toward Rosalie. He looked at Audra, blinked, and that feeling of dread in the pit of Audra's stomach dug deeper.

"He didn't come back?" Duncan replied, clearly confused.

Audra refused to panic. She absolutely could not let herself panic. She kept the placid smile on her face. Maybe he'd just been tired of chores, of having too many people in the house. Maybe he'd simply gone into Bent to *work*.

She didn't want to believe those things, but worse, she couldn't. He wouldn't have left without telling her, no matter the circumstances.

"I haven't seen him since you two left this morning," Audra said, choosing her words very carefully.

Duncan looked behind him at the door they'd left through. "He was just supposed to finish up some things while I went over to my parents'. He was going to come in for lunch."

"Lunch." That was at least two hours ago.

All eyes turned to her.

"Call Laurel," she said, very calmly, because she felt like there were two versions of herself right now. One that had flown off into the terror stratosphere, and one right here, who needed to handle the reality of whatever this was. "Tell her what we found, Franny. Tell her Copeland is missing. The cops will take it from there."

Franny scrambled for the phone on the wall, but Audra didn't stick around to listen to what she'd relay to the police.

"What are you going to do, Audra?" Rosalie asked, following at her heels as she moved to the back of the house, where her rifle safe was. Calmly and quickly, she turned the dial to unlock the safe.

"You can't go searching for him if you actually think he's in danger," Rosalie said sternly. "What happened to letting the cops handle it?"

Audra said nothing. She calmly pulled her favorite gun from the safe, then a box of bullets.

"You can't go out there, Audra. Do you hear me?"

Only once she had calmly loaded the chamber did she look at her sister. "I can. I will. I am. You can either bring your gun and join me, or you can stay here."

COPELAND HAD TO blink against the roiling sense of nausea. He was glad he hadn't passed out when he sat up, but he didn't really know the medical risks of a broken bone that wasn't seen to right away.

Of course, he had more pressing concerns. Karly Young pointing a gun at him chief among them.

"Put the gun down," she said, very calmly.

It was the calm that worried him. Calm meant…in control. It meant…planned. It meant, she knew what she was doing, and it'd be harder to talk her out of whatever she was trying to accomplish.

And it made it very hard to relinquish his one chance at stopping whatever this would be. Not that he could use his right hand to *shoot* the gun, but still.

"Stand up and move away from the gun. If you don't, the next bullet will hit its target."

"Aren't you going to kill me anyway?" Copeland asked, unwilling to let the grip on his lifeline go just yet. "Since I know you're behind everything now. And you're holding a gun on me."

Karly seemed to give this some thought, eyebrows beetled

together as she surveyed him. "I didn't want to hurt anyone," she said, still far too calm for comfort. "I just wanted what was mine. I am just taking back what *is* mine." She started to move closer, the aim of her gun squarely on his chest the entire time. "She could have just left," Karly mumbled, maybe more to herself than him. "She should have just left. It's on her now. Her fault. All her fault."

"Audra?" He almost couldn't believe what she was saying. "She… She reached out to you. She thinks of you as a sister. I watched her try to talk to you, be *kind* to you."

Karly scoffed. "You believe that? You're a sucker."

For several seconds, Copeland could only stare. He'd dealt with people who refused to engage in reality plenty, but this… It didn't make any sense. But he was starting to realize, it wouldn't. Because Karly… She wasn't dealing in reality, and she wasn't calm or collected any longer.

"I know what they are. I know what *she* is." Karly stood next to him now. He could see her chest rise and fall in exaggerated puffs. He could feel the anxious, vibrating anger coming off her. He could see the *intent*, and the wild desperation behind it, now that she was close.

Copeland didn't want to relinquish his grip on the gun, but with the broken arm, he wouldn't get a shot off aimed properly or in time anyway.

"You don't think my father told me exactly what she is?" Karly demanded. She kicked out, her heavy boot meeting both Copeland's hand and the gun. The gun went flying. New pain shot up Copeland's uninjured arm and he fell back, unable to brace his fall with his broken arm.

He laid there in the grass, feeling like a chump. He was a cop, damn it, and this unstable woman, who was trying to paint *Audra*, of all people, as some kind of villain, was winning.

He couldn't let that happen. Unable to bite back a groan of pain, he managed to sit up again. He was sweating despite the freezing temperatures, his teeth chattering now as the pain seemed to come in strange waves that were both numb and excruciating. But he met Karly's wild gaze with a calm one.

"I think you've got a lot of facts mistaken, Karly. But I think we can clear it up. If you put the gun down, if you stop trying to scare Audra…"

"You're right. I need to stop scaring." Karly was nodding now, swallowing as her eyes filled with tears. "I need to start *hurting*. The way she hurt my father."

Copeland had been in dangerous situations before, and he knew how to keep his calm. He held her gaze, and spoke low and firm. "Audra didn't do anything to your father."

"He was trapped by them!" Karly yelled. "Trapped. She was always keeping him here. It was *her*. It's all their fault. Everything he did. Every promise that didn't come true. It was *their fault*."

She'd known. Before Tim Young's death, she'd known about Audra and Rosalie and she…blamed them. And if Copeland wasn't mistaken, Tim Young had leaned into that blame. Let it fester there in his child.

Copeland didn't know how to work around that. Clearly, Karly believed it wholeheartedly, so trying to convince her otherwise wasn't going to get him anywhere.

"What about your brother?"

Karly's scowl dug deeper, but Copeland's gaze was on her other hand coming up to steady the dominant one pointing a gun at him. "Austin was *supposed* to stay put. He was *supposed* to take the fall. A little connection to *her*, and you would have picked him up in Idaho. You think *he* was smart enough to create a persona and fool that woman?"

Karly shook her head. For a second, the gun came down

a little and Copeland thought if she took one more step toward him, he could use his own legs to kick out, to catch her off guard.

"What woman?"

Karly looked at him like he was somehow completely brain-dead. "You're supposed to be a detective? That *woman*. I won't speak her name. But her connection to Austin's fake identity was supposed to lead you to *him*. She fell for it. Hook, line and sinker. Of course she did. But Austin didn't stay put. He wouldn't *listen* to what needed to be done. He didn't care about our legacy. Spoiled, spoiled, *spoiled*."

She was all but shrieking now, and she sucked in a breath. Clearly trying to center herself. The gun came back up steadily, and was aimed at his chest. "I didn't want to hurt anyone, but you all are making me."

"I'm not making you do anything, Karly," Copeland replied, keeping his voice calm as he tried to inch closer to her without her reading anything into it. As he tried to make sense of what she'd just told him. Karly was behind making Austin the internet boyfriend of Audra's mother? This wasn't just…scaring or grudges. It was full-on insanity.

So he had to keep his cool, his calm. He held Karly's wild gaze. "I just went on a horseback ride, Karly."

"You looked in to me. Not him. You kept *poking* in to *me*, not him!"

"I investigated both of you."

She curled her finger around the trigger, and Copeland stilled his movement forward. Close range, that bullet was going to end him in less than a second.

He couldn't let that happen.

"She'll come looking for you," Karly said to herself. "I bet she will. And then… I'll just have to kill all of you. I'll just have to. I don't want to, but I have to. It's mine, and it'll never really be mine if I don't kill you."

The poor woman was crying now. Copeland had been in a lot of messed-up situations, but he'd certainly never felt a modicum of pity for the person holding a gun on him.

But he did now, and it made it difficult to go after her the way he knew would save his life. "Karly, the wires got crossed somewhere." He got onto his knees, carefully, watching for any indication she might shoot. "But if we take this step by step, we can uncross them." He managed to get to his feet, even though the pain threw off his balance. He held his hands in the air, a sign of surrender, even though he wasn't surrendering. "And no one has to get hurt. I promise you. No one has to get hurt."

Karly stared at him, tears streaming down her cheeks. "You believe that," she said, almost like it was a revelation. But then she shook her head. "What a shame you believe that."

Chapter Twenty-One

Audra didn't bother to wait and see if Rosalie was keeping up. She had one mission. Get to the back side of the property.

She was certain that was where Copeland was. He was either digging into things alone, in which case she might shoot him herself. Or he was…

She threw that *or* away. Let the terrified version of her deal with it. Right now, there was only getting to him and figuring out what was what.

The answer came before she reached the back of the property. She heard the pounding of hooves, looked over to one of the pastures, where Bo was running in a kind of endless circle.

Bo. The horse Copeland took when he rode with her. Audra swallowed. She wanted to run, but that would only scare Bo even more. She approached, in careful steady strides, speaking in low, calming tones.

"Whoa. Whoa." She managed to approach Bo, grab her reins even as she reared back up. Audra stayed out of the way as the horse came back onto all fours. "It's all right, sweetheart. I've got you now." But she didn't have time…

Rosalie caught up, and so did Duncan and Franny, who Audra hadn't realized had followed them out.

Franny moved forward, took the reins from Audra. "I've got her," Franny said firmly. "I've got her. I'll be okay. You guys go."

Audra took off, but Rosalie was right behind, talking to Duncan. "You two go back to the house. Get Bo put away. Then you can lead the cops to us once they get here."

"Rosalie." Duncan's voice was little more than a growl, but Rosalie kept pace with Audra and just spoke louder.

"We can handle it, Duncan. We have to handle it. Go with Franny. Please."

Audra didn't pay any attention to see if Duncan argued or not. She kept resolutely walking to the back of the property. She could have grabbed a horse—Bo, even—but she wasn't sure Bo was okay, and any other horse would take too long to saddle. Her truck could have made it back here, but she would have had to backtrack. The UTV was out of gas, so on foot it was.

"Audra…" But Rosalie never finished whatever she was going to say. She just kept up with Audra's relentless, determined pace. Over hills and dips, along the fence line and to the back of the property.

Maybe Audra was breathing heavily from exertion as they began to approach the end of her property line, but she hardly noticed. Out there in the distance, she saw a figure.

No, two figures.

Only when she saw the sun glint off the metal of what was likely a gun did she begin to slow. But she didn't stop.

Because she could see clearly one figure was standing with his hands in the air—that was Copeland. And one figure held a gun toward him—that was Karly.

If it meant something, if she felt something, it didn't penetrate the icy shell inside of her. The only thing she really concentrated on was a renewed sense of determination. She lifted her rifle as she walked closer.

"Audra, we should try to sneak up on her. We should—"

"There's nowhere to hide," Audra replied. Because all

around them was just the rolling grassy land of Young Ranch and the spot they'd sold off to the lumber company with years-old stumps lining the ground.

Whether it was their voices or something else, Audra didn't know, but Karly looked toward them, the gun still pointed at Copeland. Audra thought she'd turn it toward her and Rosalie, considering they were armed, but Karly didn't do that.

She stepped closer to Copeland, behind him almost, but not fully. Because she pressed the metal to his temple.

Audra stopped on a dime, but she didn't lower her gun. She didn't feel panic or terror or worry. She was so calm, everything around her felt like some...unreal dream. She could feel Rosalie behind her, but all she saw, all she felt, was the calm dark gaze of Copeland from across the grassy expanse between them.

"Audra." Rosalie sounded scared, but Audra didn't feel it. She was numb. She was calm. She knew what had to be done.

She kept Karly in her gunsight. "I'm going to shoot her," Audra murmured.

"She's using Copeland as a shield."

"I can see that. I can also see exactly where I need to aim to hit her and not Copeland."

"But... Audra, what if you hit him?" Rosalie asked on a concerned whisper.

Audra's hand wanted to tremble, but she wouldn't let it. For years, she'd won shooting awards. Hell, she'd helped save the ranch with the money she won a few years in a row. Now she'd help save the man she loved.

"I won't hit him." Not when everything depended on this. On her.

She'd been preparing for this moment, whether she knew it or not, all her life.

THE GUN WAS pressed to his temple. Copeland had no doubt Karly would pull the trigger if pushed even a little bit. She was holding on to everything by a thread. He could *feel* her desperation. Her loss of control, and maybe loss of hope that she could turn this whole messed-up endeavor into what she'd envisioned.

Audra didn't look the least bit scared. She held the impressive-looking rifle against her shoulder, aimed at…well, he knew it wasn't aimed at *him*, but it sure felt like it with Karly using him as a human shield.

If Audra had any feelings about that, she didn't show it. The sun blazed behind her in a riot of deep reds and oranges. Her expression was calm, her eyes direct.

"Drop the gun," Karly called out over the distance between them. "You've got ten seconds, or he's gone."

Audra's gaze didn't move. The gun didn't drop. Her finger was curled around the trigger. Karly was on his right side, so his arm couldn't do much. He could maybe land a kick before *she* shot him, but he didn't know what the hell Audra's plans were.

Karly started counting, but Copeland couldn't pay attention. He was focused on Audra. Her blue eyes were on her target, and they didn't waver.

She was going to shoot…and whatever happened, well, he'd have to deal with it.

When the gunshot went off, Copeland didn't even flinch. The gun fell from his temple, exploded loudly near his ear, but he didn't feel any impact. He turned to Karly.

She'd fallen backward, and she was screaming…though it was muffled to his ears. Her hand was bloody, but even as she shouted and cried, she was trying to reach out for her dropped gun with her left hand.

Copeland scooped it up easily before she did with *his* left hand. Karly was screaming at him, but he couldn't make out the words. The gunshot had exploded too close to his ear.

Then he felt arms come around him. He couldn't hold back the groan of pain or stop himself from swaying. Audra held him firm though, and he wrapped his good arm around her.

She was saying something to him, though he couldn't make it out. But he got the drift when she started searching him for signs of injury or blood maybe.

"I'm okay. I'm not shot. I just took a tumble off Bo. Hurt my arm a bit." His own words sounded weird and muffled. Audra's blue eyes were bright with tears, but they didn't fall. Rosalie appeared, holding a gun pointed at Karly.

Both Rosalie and Audra were saying things, but he couldn't make out the words, so he just squeezed Audra tighter, trying to ignore the pain. "Gun went off a little close to my ear, so it's all a bit muffled right now." Easier to admit that when she looked so worried than that his arm was broken.

"Audra." He looked at Karly, still writhing on the ground with Rosalie holding her at gunpoint, then at Audra, who only seemed to have eyes for him. He had to tell her. "It was Karly all along. She knew about you guys, this place, and I think... I think your father convinced her it was all your fault you had this and she didn't." He spoke in low tones, keeping his good arm tight around her. "She was just trying to frame Austin for it. Down to the fake identity catfishing your mother."

Audra watched him as he spoke. *Dazed* wasn't the right word. She just seemed detached. Or partially detached, because he thought the emotion was starting to break through.

The muffled sound and pain in his ear were starting to ease a little, he thought, when he heard the faint sound of sirens.

It was when the police cruiser and the ambulance crested the rise that Audra began to shake. Then a tear slid onto her cheek.

He squeezed her tight. "Baby, you held that gun steady and shot somebody with about a centimeter of wiggle room. I don't think you get to fall apart now."

She pressed her forehead into his shoulder. She was still shaking, but he didn't know if she was actively crying since she'd hidden her face. "Sure," she said, her voice squeaky, even to his muffled hearing. "I'll just keep it together then."

"You kept it together when it counted." He pressed a kiss to her temple. "Hell, Audra. I don't know anyone who could have made that shot. Not a soul. Except you."

Chapter Twenty-Two

Audra gave her statement to Laurel while they loaded Copeland into the ambulance. She allowed herself to be fussed over by Rosalie and Franny, all while Copeland was taken to the hospital.

And she cursed the man when Laurel informed her he was going into surgery for a broken arm. "He knew it was broken," she told Rosalie darkly back at their kitchen table with cops prowling the property. "He knew it the whole time and didn't tell me."

"Well, we'll go down to the hospital and you can yell at him about it."

Audra frowned, because she wasn't going to yell at him. The minute she saw him, she'd probably fall completely apart. His words kept echoing in her head.

I don't know anyone who could have made that shot. Not a soul. Except you.

Like somehow, it was all meant to be. Like somehow, she shouldn't feel guilty about asking Copeland for help, about his broken arm he'd got because of *her*.

She did, of course, feel guilty and blamed herself, but there was a little inkling deep down that maybe she *shouldn't*.

Still, once the police presence moved out, she let Rosalie drive her to the hospital because she needed to see Copeland. She wouldn't take a full breath until she did.

It was late by the time they got to the hospital and made their way toward Copeland's recovery room. Before they reached it though, they saw Laurel talking to a uniformed police officer outside a hospital room at the front of the hall.

The two stopped talking as Rosalie and Audra walked by.

Rosalie studied them, then the door. "Is it Karly?" she demanded.

Laurel gave them a kind of cop smile. Sympathetic but guarded. "She's doing just fine. She'll likely have some permanent damage, since the wrist is a hell of a place to get shot, but she'll make a full recovery. And then we'll see about justice."

"Can we see her?" Audra asked, without fully thinking the question through. Everything just felt…so unsettled, even with what Copeland had told her.

Laurel looked from Rosalie to Audra, then back to the uniformed officer outside the hospital-room door.

"It'll be up to her. I'll go see if she's okay with it, and I'll have to stay in the room with you."

Audra nodded, and Laurel slipped into the room.

Rosalie turned to Audra, concern etched across her features. "Why?"

"I don't know. It just seems… Dad convinced her of all this stuff that wasn't true, and she was acting on it in good faith."

Rosalie scowled. "She would have killed Copeland. And possibly you. Even if she believed every lie Dad ever told, that's not an excuse for *murder.*"

"She had chances to do both and didn't."

Rosalie shook her head. "I don't know how you can have any sympathy for her, Aud. She's a damn criminal."

"She's troubled. She needs help. She's our sister."

Maybe, just maybe, that softened Rosalie a little. When

Laurel reappeared and ushered them into the room, Rosalie linked arms with Audra. They stopped at the end of Karly's hospital bed.

She was hooked up to an IV and some other kind of machine. Her gaze slowly landed on them, settled on their linked arms while a scowl sank into her face.

"Well. What do you two want?" she said it with a sneer. "If you're expecting an apology, you can jump off a cliff. *You* shot me."

Audra supposed it should make her mad, but all she could seem to work up to was sympathy. To be this…angry at all the wrong people. It was just sad.

"I'm sorry it was the only option," Audra said, and meant it. "But I think we both know you were ready to kill someone, and that's just…not okay."

Karly's belligerent gaze moved out to the window, even though it was dark outside, and her jaw worked, like she was trying to hold back tears. Like she *knew*, deep down, what she'd done was wrong.

Maybe it was wishful thinking, but Audra, who'd given up on wishful thinking since her father had died, decided she wanted some of that hope, some of that belief back.

"I would have given you a piece of the ranch," Audra said very calmly and clearly. "I would have given you so much. I offered. You didn't even consider my offer."

Karly stared at her. There was hate deep in the eyes the same shade as Audra's, but Audra thought she saw something else. Maybe she was fooling herself, but she hoped she saw some doubt.

So she pressed. "*He* tricked you. He tricked all of us. He's the enemy. And if you can ever accept that, believe it, I'll be here."

"We'll be here," Rosalie corrected, surprising Audra. Because her sister wasn't exactly known for her forgiving nature.

Karly still said nothing. She would do some time. Hopefully she'd get some help, and maybe someday in the future they could put this behind them.

But if they didn't, at least Audra tried.

"Whatever," Karly muttered. "Go away."

Audra exchanged a glance with Rosalie, who nodded. They'd done what they needed to do for some closure, and left the door cracked open if Karly ever decided to step through it.

COPELAND SWAM OUT of the dark in a weird fuzzy kind of confusion. He didn't feel much of anything, least of all his body, but when his eyes opened to a bright, white hospital room he was met by a familiar dark gaze.

He stared for a full minute before it made sense. "Mom?"

His mother was frowning disapprovingly at him from a seat next to his hospital bed. "Well, who else would be here?"

Copeland shifted uncomfortably, not sure if it was the anesthesia from surgery wearing off or what. "You didn't have to come all the way here."

"My son was in surgery and I didn't have to come all the way here." She scoffed. "Leave it to you, Copeland."

He might have laughed, but his brain didn't feel like it was firing on all cylinders yet. "I..." He wanted—needed—to see Audra. They'd wheeled him into surgery before he'd had a chance to talk to her, they'd both been so busy giving statements and ensuring the loose ends of Karly Young had been tied up.

Now he wanted... God, he just wanted to see her. But his mother was here. She'd come all the way from Denver and... "Mom, it's just a broken arm."

She made a considering noise. "We were overdue for a visit. For seeing your life here. I know you've come home, but why shouldn't we come here for a bit? Good for your father to get away from his precious lawn for a week or so."

See your life here. No, he'd kept them away from it. Hell, he'd tried to keep himself away from life, but he'd built one all the same. No matter what he'd tried to do. It hadn't started with Audra, but it all seemed to center on her now and... His parents were *here*. So...

"I'd like you to meet someone."

"It wouldn't happen to be a pretty woman named Audra who introduced herself to me as the reason you got hurt?"

He sighed heavily. Martyr until the end. "That'd be her. It wasn't her fault."

"You don't think I know that? Sometimes it's easier for people to take the blame and feel in control of everything that's hurting their heart, than it is to accept bad things just happen."

Maybe he'd realized that a bit on his own, but his mother articulating it clarified all that martyr in her. And maybe even a little in himself.

"She's helping your dad hunt down some decent coffee," Mom continued, her gaze shrewd. "She's a sweet girl. First impression? I liked her."

"Good." Maybe it was the drugs. The exhaustion. Maybe it was just seeing his mother here in Wyoming. But the truth came tumbling out. "Because I think I'm in love with her."

Mom didn't react outwardly, but he saw her gaze study him, like she could see through him and determined it was true. "My suggestion would be not to use the word *think* when you tell her. Your father made that mistake. I nearly ended things then and there."

He laughed in spite of himself. "Noted."

But he saw, or felt, his mother's…concern. Trepidation maybe. Because he'd run away from one problem, and maybe she was worried he was just repeating old mistakes. So he felt like he had to tell her, had to explain…

"It's not just her, you know. It's this place. It's a community. I have friends. No matter how hard I tried, everything, everyone…became more than just a job. More than just an escape from Denver. I left to…hide, I guess. Numb myself. But…"

She reached out, brushed his hair off his forehead, just like she'd done when he'd been a kid home sick from school. "But it sounds like you found your home instead."

"Yeah, I think I did."

"That's all I ever wanted for you," she said, and though her expression was calm, her eyes filled a little. But she didn't cry. She wouldn't—that wasn't his mother's way.

She cleared her throat. They both turned to look as the door to the room opened. Dad stepped in first, but he was followed by Audra. She had shadows under her eyes. She needed rest and home and…

She was here, and that was exactly where he wanted her to be.

"We're going to stay a few days," Mom said briskly. "Until you're out of the hospital at least. No arguing. We're going to go check into the hotel now. We'll be back in the morning." She reached out, took Audra's hand. "It was good to meet you, Audra. I'm sure we'll see more of you before we leave."

Audra smiled in return. "I hope so."

For a second, Copeland watched his parents and Audra and wondered if this was all a very elaborate dream. But then Audra sat in the chair next to his bed. She reached out, touched his face, and that touch was real.

He felt himself relax into the pillows beneath his head.

Real. All this was real, and once he was out of here, it'd be time to figure out just what that meant.

"Your parents are very nice," she said, a bit primly, but he knew she was trying to keep herself from apologizing about his arm.

"Yeah, they are."

"How are you feeling?"

"Weird. Groggy. But okay. Guess I've got desk duty for a bit."

She glanced at his cast, pain and no doubt a bit of self-flagellation there in her gaze, but she didn't speak it. That was progress, he thought.

"I'm not going to tell you I'm sorry," she said, very clearly struggling with that. "But only because your mother told me not to."

He laughed at that, for so many reasons. He shook his head. "Audra, you are something else. I'm just glad you're safe, and we got to the bottom of it, no matter how accidentally. I wish I could have done more, sooner, but we're okay. And... Hopefully Karly can get the help she needs."

Audra's mouth turned down. "But...she tried to kill you. She was going to. You don't have some sort of...revenge feeling about that?"

"Normally I would, but... I don't know. She just seemed so damn sad. It was impossible not to feel sorry for her."

Audra swallowed, her eyes swimming again. She got up out of the chair just enough to brush a light kiss across his mouth. "I thought so too." She offered him a trembling smile.

And he just...said it, because it was there, and it should be said. She should hear it. Know it. Always. He didn't even use the word *think*.

"I'm in love with you, Audra, and believe me, that was *not* the plan."

She kind of plunked back into her seat, shock etched across her face. She opened her mouth, but nothing came out. So he figured he'd just press and press and press while he could.

She was stubborn. He'd have to get through to her.

"Guess I'll be laid up for a few weeks, but I make a pretty good ranch hand."

She swallowed. "You do. Cheap too."

"Audra."

She sighed, gaze lifting from his cast to his face. Her blue eyes were tired, soft. "I always wanted… I wanted to fall in love. To find someone who felt like a partner. I chased that feeling, and it only ever broke my heart. So I wasn't looking for you either. I was done chasing. Done…believing." She took a long, careful inhale. "But you're worth believing in, Copeland. And I love you."

For a few moments they just stared at each other, like the moment was nebulous, fragile, breakable.

Then Audra laughed, got up again, and pressed a firmer kiss to his mouth.

He held her there with his good arm before she could sit back down. "You're going to have a hell of a hard time getting rid of me, I hope you know that."

She smiled, pretty and bright, just like she was, all the way through. "Good."

* * * * *

Get up to 4 Free Books!

We'll send you 2 free books from each series you try
PLUS a free Mystery Gift.

FREE
Value Over
$25

Both the **Harlequin Intrigue®** and **Harlequin® Romantic Suspense** series
feature compelling novels filled with heart-racing action-packed romance
that will keep you on the edge of your seat.

YES! Please send me 2 FREE novels from the Harlequin Intrigue or Harlequin Romantic Suspense series and my FREE gift (gift is worth about $10 retail). After receiving them, if I don't wish to receive any more books, I can return the shipping statement marked "cancel." If I don't cancel, I will receive 6 brand-new Harlequin Intrigue Larger-Print books every month and be billed just $7.19 each in the U.S. or $7.99 each in Canada, or 4 brand-new Harlequin Romantic Suspense books every month and be billed just $6.39 each in the U.S. or $7.19 each in Canada, a savings of 20% off the cover price. It's quite a bargain! Shipping and handling is just 50¢ per book in the U.S. and $1.25 per book in Canada.* I understand that accepting the 2 free books and gift places me under no obligation to buy anything. I can always return a shipment and cancel at any time by calling the number below. The free books and gift are mine to keep no matter what I decide.

Choose one:
- ☐ **Harlequin Intrigue Larger-Print** (199/399 BPA G36Y)
- ☐ **Harlequin Romantic Suspense** (240/340 BPA G36Y)
- ☐ **Or Try Both!** (199/399 & 240/340 BPA G36Z)

Name (please print)

Address   Apt. #

City   State/Province   Zip/Postal Code

Email: Please check this box ☐ if you would like to receive newsletters and promotional emails from Harlequin Enterprises ULC and its affiliates. You can unsubscribe anytime.

Mail to the Harlequin Reader Service:
IN U.S.A.: P.O. Box 1341, Buffalo, NY 14240-8531
IN CANADA: P.O. Box 603, Fort Erie, Ontario L2A 5X3

Want to explore our other series or interested in ebooks? Visit www.ReaderService.com or call 1-800-873-8635.

HIHRS25